MISADVENTURES IN BLUE

BY
SIERRA SIMONE

MISADVENTURES IN BLUE

BY
SIERRA SIMONE

This book is an original publication of Waterhouse Press.

Cover Design by Waterhouse Press.
Cover images: Shutterstock

PRINTED IN THE UNITED STATES OF AMERICA

ISBN: 978-1-64263-140-1

To Josh, for all these years of couch time.
I love you.

CHAPTER ONE

JACE

A burglary sounds more exciting than it is.

Burglars are opportunists, generally, and the ones smart enough to do it more than once are smart enough to know how to do it right. Know what you want and take it while no one else is around.

Sticking a gun in a bank teller's face isn't going to get you anything but a prison sentence—but if we're talking the kind of theft that happens without anyone getting hurt? And for shit that isn't federally protected? Well, be clever and you might just get away with it.

Anyway, alarm calls for business structures at night usually turn out to be nothing. Bad wiring or teens goofing off or—most commonly—a night cleaning crew with an old alarm code. And the turns-out-to-be-nothing calls are frequent enough that I'm surprised when I get to the scene and actually find broken glass everywhere. A brief and welcome shot of adrenaline pulses through me as I call it in and draw my weapon to search the premises.

Empty.

With a disappointment that is as irrational as it is

unwanted, I update dispatch and call my sergeant.

"Russo," she answers in her usual clipped way.

"Hey, Sarge, it's Sutton. I'm responding to that alarm at 10533 Mastin, and I think you should call Detective Day in. It looks like another one of her doctor's office robberies."

I can tell by the pause on the other end of the phone that my sergeant has no idea what I'm talking about.

"She sent an email about it last week," I add. "Asking to be alerted if there was another one, which I think this is."

I hear clicking and sighing and guess that Russo is double-checking her own inbox to find Detective Day's email.

"All right, kid," Russo says. "Found the email. Looks like calling her in is what we need to do."

That at least gives me some kind of satisfaction. Maybe there is no one to chase, nothing to *do,* but at least I can make sure the right person gets the right information.

But it isn't a lot of satisfaction.

Well, Jace, what did you expect when you took a job working for a suburban police department? Firefights? Car chases?

No. I knew exactly what I was doing when I applied at Hocker Grove Police Department. My sister just had her second baby, my folks were retiring, and I wanted to put down roots. I wanted to buy a house and maybe get my degree and settle down. I wanted something more than the stop-and-start life of active duty in the army like I had before.

I wanted to come back to the place where I grew up.

I walk out of the doctor's office and crunch across the broken glass back to my car for the crime-scene tape, taking in the typical Hocker Grove night as I do. I take in the empty parking lot, still puddled and damp from an earlier storm and lit by lonely light poles, and I take in the distant roar of the interstate and the rustling of wet tree leaves in the wind.

I smell the suburban air, a mix of wet grass and gasoline. The almost-country and the almost-city mixed together.

I smell home.

Although for being home sweet suburban home, Hocker Grove is plenty busy and plenty grim. As the second-most-populous city in the state of Kansas, with almost two hundred thousand people, every type of crime comes out to play. Domestic abuse, drug abuse, battery, assault, theft, and so many auto burglaries that they have their own unit in the investigation division.

As I know from my own childhood growing up in a shitty apartment tucked behind a Walmart, Hocker Grove isn't all happy middle-class families and prosperity. But even with all the work that needs to be done, the pace of life here after six years in the army and three hellish stints in Afghanistan feels, well...boring and uneventful.

Russo arrives right as I am pulling the tape from my car, and after her come Coulson, Romero, and Quinn. Together it doesn't take long to get the scene roped off and secure, and afterward, I slide into my car and start sketching out the beginnings of my report. I hate paperwork, but if there's one thing I learned from the army, it's that there's no point in putting off things you hate. *Especially* paperwork. It just bites you in the ass harder when the time comes.

"I heard they called in the Ice Queen," Quinn says, coming over to lean against my car and talking to me through my open window. Quinn's fresh out of field training, like me, but a couple of years younger, and sometimes that couple of years feels like decades.

But as my grandmother used to say, I'm an old soul, and I'm sure fighting in a literal war did nothing to make that soul any younger. So I take a deep breath and try to be patient with the fact that this guy wants to shoot the shit while all I want is to get my work done.

"Ice Queen?" I ask, not looking up from the report screen of the mounted tablet in the car.

"Yeah, man. Cat Day. You haven't heard about her?"

I could point out that in a department of nearly four hundred commissioned officers, there are a lot of people I haven't heard of, but I don't bother. Quinn doesn't need my help keeping a conversation going.

"So get this. Years and years ago, she was engaged to another cop, and he was killed in the line of duty. Killed *right in front of her*. And when the other officers arrived on the scene, they found her sitting on the steps outside the house where he was killed and she's covered in his blood from trying to do CPR, and the first thing she says is, 'Can I wash my hands?'"

He pauses for effect. I keep typing.

He keeps going, with more hand gestures now, to drive home his point. "Not 'Oh my God, my fiancé is fucking dead' or 'Someone wheel me to the psych ward because I just watched the man I love bleed out' or anything like that. Nope. 'Can I wash my hands?' She wasn't even *crying*. And they said she never did cry, like ever, not even at his funeral. How messed up is that?"

Honestly, I don't think it's messed up at all.

Everyone reacts to trauma differently. I once saved a civilian's life by shoving my fingers into an open wound in his thigh, and three hours later I was eating nachos in the DFAC and complaining about how the Chiefs couldn't get their shit together. The only way to keep living after these moments is to focus on the tiny realities that, when stitched together, make life normal. Washing your hands. Nachos. Talking about things that don't matter.

To stay normal you have to pretend to be normal.

It's compartmentalization—but you can't say that word to the therapists and counselors because then they start nodding and writing stuff down.

"Who's *they*?" I ask, looking up from my tablet.

Quinn's red-blond brows furrow together. "What do you mean?"

"You said *they* are saying this stuff about Detective Day. Who?"

He waves an impatient hand. "It's just like—stories, man. Gossip and stuff."

"Why does anyone care?"

"Because she's still, like, a frigid bitch," Quinn states as if it's obvious.

His words piss me off. "That's unprofessional to say," I tell him. "Not to mention shitty."

Quinn rolls his eyes and his body at the same time in a kind of *oh come ON* gesture. "You're no fun, Sutton."

"So I've heard," I say, getting back to the report.

"Ugh. Fine. But mark my words when you meet her. Frig—"

I give him an irritated glare, and he finally, thankfully, shuts up and leaves me alone.

Ice Queen.

I wonder what she's actually like. My mom was a firefighter, and I know being a woman and a first responder means walking along a wire with no safety net. Too passive and you get ignored for promotions and recognition. Too aggressive and you get labeled a bitch. Act like a man and you'll succeed—but then you'll be punished for not being enough like a woman.

This reflection, along with random thoughts about being home and being bored, filter through my mind as a civilian car rolls into the parking lot. A very nice civilian car.

I watch with interest as it coasts into a spot and stops and then with even more interest as a woman climbs out in a blouse and skirt—no uniform, although there is a badge clipped to the waist of her skirt.

Detective Catherine Day.

She's slender, upright, with posture and movements so graceful that there must be ballet shoes in her past...ski trips and horses too. Light-blond hair waves just past her shoulders, sleek and glamorous in that Old Hollywood kind of way, and the drape of her silk blouse and the fitted hug of her pencil skirt scream money and delicacy and restraint.

She is sophistication embodied.

And all of this refined dignity is coupled with a direct, determined stride and quick, efficient assessments of her surroundings. She exudes confidence. Independence. Power.

I don't know about the *ice* part, but the *queen*?

Yes. I can sense it from here.

In the thirty seconds it takes her to tuck her leather portfolio against her stomach and walk into the building, Catherine Day obliterates any thoughts of boredom or disappointment, and I feel a strange jolt of unhappiness when she walks out of my sight.

I close out my tablet with a few impatient stabs and get out of my car. Talking to her is the only thing I want to do.

CHAPTER TWO

CAT

I'll never concede that crime scenes and high heels don't mix.

I duck under the yellow tape to find the on-duty sergeant and notice a spray of broken glass on the ground. With a rueful glance down at my nude Manolo Blahniks, I pick my way carefully through the sparkling debris to the woman facing away from me, talking into the radio on her shoulder. I've never been more grateful for my years of ballet and yoga as I am when I make it to her with my balance and dignity intact.

Sergeant Russo gives me a friendly—if slightly disbelieving—once-over as I reach her, eyeing my silk blouse and tailored pencil skirt. A sleek leather portfolio is tucked under my elbow.

"Just rolled out of bed like that, huh?" she asks, letting go of her radio and gesturing for me to follow her through a doorway to the real crime scene.

I smile as we walk in, but I don't answer. Nicki Russo and I went through academy together, and while we're friends, her remarks about my clothes have always been more than a little pointed. *Detective Dry Clean Only* is her favorite nickname for me—which I suppose is nicer than the one they call me when

I'm not around.

Officer Ice Queen.

They've been calling me that since Frazer's funeral twelve years ago. The funeral where I didn't cry, didn't mourn, didn't expose a single sliver of the raw, howling pain I actually felt.

"Tell me what we've got," I say, setting aside the sharp memories and taking in the scene. "Same as last time?"

Russo nods. "Even down to the timing. Doctor's office, hit after ten. The window around the door is broken—likely what triggered the alarm. We had a uniform here within seven minutes. He searched the office and the rest of the building. No one in sight."

I look around the half-lit waiting room. There's glass from the broken window out on the sidewalk and a spray of shards glinting on the carpet. The usual array of pointless, uninteresting magazines are still neatly arranged on the tables, and the corner houses a collection of wooden toys. Except for the glass, it could be any well-kept, undisturbed waiting room, all but—

"The television again," I murmur, finding what I was looking for. A bare TV mount on the wall, random wires and cords dangling from the ceiling above it.

"Yep," Russo agrees. "My guy saw it right away. He was the one who told me to call you, by the way. Actually read your email about it all."

"And you didn't read my email?" I ask absently, walking up to the wall and examining the mount.

"Do you know how many emails I get in a day?" asks Russo.

It's a rhetorical question, so I don't bother answering, but I do say, "That was attentive of your officer to remember it. I'd like to speak with him, if I may."

"Sure. And the office manager is here too. She might be able to give you a preliminary report of what's missing."

"Nothing else will be missing," I say, more to myself than Russo, still looking at the mount. It was poorly installed, and drywall dust litters the carpet below, as if dislodging the television from the mount sent a shower of the stuff everywhere. "They just want the TVs."

A string of similar robberies has plagued the city for the past two months. It's always doctors' offices, it's always TVs, and it's always at night.

I normally work in crimes against persons—homicide, stalking, assault—but my experience working a similar case for the Kansas Bureau of Investigation a few years back had my sergeant pulling me to work this one. I don't mind, since my usual caseload is a lot grimmer than stolen televisions, but it has been unexpectedly frustrating.

I have one of the highest case clearance rates in the department; I'm not used to failing. Yet I've been on this one for four solid weeks with nothing to show for it.

It's galling, and an unfamiliar itch of restlessness works its way down my spine. It's everything I can do to maintain my poise as I turn back to Russo.

"The scene techs are taking pictures?"

"Already done. They're working on trying to lift prints now, but good luck with a fucking waiting room, you know?"

I make an agreeing kind of noise as we head back toward

the scheduling desks, where a wan young woman stands next to a copier. She looks stunned, a confused kind of afraid, and a frisson of impatience skates through me.

There are far worse things than a stolen television—particularly one stolen when no one was around—and I want to tell her that. I want to tell her she doesn't realize what horrors life can present. What fears. Even when Frazer died, I still managed to keep my pain and terror and guilt locked safely inside—

I stop the train of thought immediately. It's not helping the strange restless itch burrowing deeper and deeper into my chest. An itch that seems to be equal parts vexation over the case and some indefinable physical need.

I take a subtle breath, remind myself that this girl is probably in her early twenties and that I don't need to infect her with my jaded, thirty-seven-year-old weariness.

"I'm Detective Catherine Day," I say, extending my hand.

She looks at it for a moment, lost, and then seems to remember what's expected and shakes it. "Gia," she replies.

Russo grins at her. "Good Italian name."

"Uh, yeah. Pisani. Last name." She lets out a huffy little laugh, as if realizing how wooden she's being. "Sorry. This is just so weird."

I give her a small smile. "We'll need you to submit a complete list of everything missing or disturbed in the office, Gia, but whatever you can tell me now will be helpful for the initial report."

She shakes her head, looking lost. "It's only the television... It's bewildering. It's just *gone*."

"But no one was hurt," Russo tells her. "And in the grand scheme of things, a TV is not the worst thing they could have taken. They could have taken medicine to sell off or all sorts of expensive medical equipment."

Gia chews her lip. "You're right, of course. Absolutely right. It's just this is my first real job out of college, and I have no idea what to do or if it's somehow my fault..."

I catch her uncertain gaze, touching her elbow as I do. "It's not your fault, and I'll guide you through as much of this as I can."

With Gia somewhat mollified, I manage to get a decent preliminary interview out of her, arrange for a follow-up later this week, and ask for a complete inventory of the equipment and other valuable items in the office. Then Russo and I head back outside to the parking lot to find the responding officer.

"*Bewildering*," Russo echoes. "Can you imagine using the word 'bewildering' out loud?"

"The diploma over her desk was from Vassar," I say a bit distractedly, feeling a short buzz from my phone and looking down to check it. Even with the parking lot lights sending a diffused glow over the pavement, the screen is painfully bright after I tap the notification open. "Maybe she's simply well-spoken. Excuse me. I need to check this."

Russo stops and politely waits for me to check my latest email. I register a small click of satisfaction when I see it's something I've been waiting for.

"Boyfriend?" Russo asks, noticing my pleased expression.

"Crime Analysis," I reply. "Extracted data from the license plate readers in the area of the last burglary."

She rolls her eyes. "Day, you need a boyfriend. Or a girlfriend. You can't fuck extracted data, or at least so I've heard."

"I'm fine, Nicki."

She gives me a mock scowl at the use of her first name. "You seem fine, *Cat*. Really, really, superduper fine."

We're angling toward a clump of officers standing next to a patrol car. Even in the dark, they've all got the requisite patrol cop sunglasses propped on their heads, and every last one of them has a gas station coffee cup clutched in one hand—vital medicine for any officer on any shift, day or night.

"I *am* fine. I promise."

She softens, going from friendly ribbing to the earnest tomboy I met fifteen years ago at academy. "Frazer would want you to be happy, you know," she says quietly enough that the uniforms can't hear her as we approach. "He wouldn't want you to live like this...married to the job since you couldn't marry him."

My chest tightens uncomfortably.

It's been twelve years since he died, and there's been plenty of therapy and life between then and now and still her words sting. I tuck my phone carefully inside my portfolio, swallow, and say, "I'm happy, Nicki. Truly."

It's a lie, but she doesn't press me on it, for which I'm grateful. "Okay," she says. "I just want to see you have a little fun is all. Live a little."

"I know. And thank you."

She gives my shoulder a little shove, a playful gesture literally no one else in the department would attempt with me, and then we're to the chattering cops and the conversation is over.

The restless itch, however, is back, tickling between my shoulder blades and tugging deep in my belly. Damn her, but Russo's words have gotten under my skin.

Am I lonely? Am I married to my job and starving myself of happiness?

Of course not. How ridiculous.

But if it's so ridiculous, why this itch? Why this feeling like I'm waiting for something, missing something? Or someone?

"Sutton," Russo calls out. "Someone here to talk to you."

One of the uniforms breaks away from the knot of gossiping cops and turns toward us. He's young—very young—no more than twenty-three or twenty-four, but he's without the swagger most cops have at that age. And it's obvious he doesn't need it.

Serious gray eyes stare out from under equally serious brows. A slightly Grecian nose leads to a sculpted mouth currently pressed into a solemn, no-nonsense line—which only serves to highlight the tempting peaks of his upper lip and the subtle fullness of the lower even more.

His high-and-tight haircut is relaxed just enough that I could run my fingers through the dark thickness at the top but still short enough to show off his uplifted cheekbones and strong jaw. And his body—his body is pure sex. Young, vigorous, twenty-something sex. Broad shoulders testing the seams of his uniform shirt arrow down into trim hips neatly circled by a duty belt. His uniform pants cling to hard, athletic thighs, and right below his belt, there's the bulge of a mouthwatering cock at rest. Oh God, oh God—

I blush, my eyes snapping back up to his face. There's no way he didn't see me giving him such an obvious once-over. Except he doesn't look proud or amused—the two reactions I'd expect from a hotshot-looking rookie.

He looks thoughtful. And maybe a little curious.

"Sutton, this is Cat Day. She's the lead detective on these robberies."

"I remember," he says. His voice is deep and rough—just like sex with him would be—and at hearing it, something behind my sternum pulls free with enough force to make my lips part on a silent gasp, and heat spills from my chest to my belly to somewhere lower down.

That itch from earlier is resolving itself into thudding, hot aches everywhere. Everywhere I thought my body had gone quiet over the years. The tips of my breasts, the neglected bundle of nerves between my legs. My lips and my fingertips and even the skin of my belly, all craving heat and friction. All craving *him*. His combination of strength and power and youth—that thrill of seeing a man so young and virile vibrate with such restrained intensity.

Now is when I should speak, when I should take control of the situation again, but I can't trust my voice not to betray the sudden, purring desire currently humming across the surface of my skin. Instead, I extend a hand for a quick, professional shake.

His hand is larger than mine, warm and dry and calloused, and the moment our skin touches, I know it was a mistake. Electricity sizzles through me, and with his eyes locked on mine as we touch, it's impossible not to imagine that gray gaze on me as he pumps between my legs. Staring down at me as I take his heavy cock into my mouth. Touching him, no matter how professionally, only drives me to further distraction.

"Nice to meet you." That *voice.* Even listening to him, no matter how bland the words are, feels like a prurient act—like I shouldn't be doing it in public. Surely everyone around us can see how my skin is catching fire? How my nipples are beading through my lace bra and silk blouse?

"Nice to meet you," I manage back, praying I sound composed. "I appreciate you making sure I was brought in tonight."

"I read your email," he explains and then says nothing else. A man of few words, I suppose, although there's no mistaking the intensity at which he operates. It's in his extreme focus, the predatory stillness of his form. In the tension around his mouth and the alert tilts of his head.

It's hard to mind either the silence or the intensity when his eyes are shimmering mercury in the hazy radiance of the parking lot lights. They're the kind of eyes that seem to say everything his mouth won't, and it's next to impossible to tear myself away when Russo breaks in and asks me a question.

"Hey, do you need Sutton much longer? He's an evenings boy, and his shift finished an hour ago."

Right.

Shifts. Robberies.

Police work.

Focus, Cat. Work the case.

"Only a few minutes more, Nicki," I tell her and then turn

to Sutton. "Do you mind going over what you found with me?"

The shake of his head is deliberate, precise. No motion wasted, no emotion betrayed. "Whatever you need."

God. I could listen to that voice say *whatever you need* every night for the rest of my life. Low in my ear...against the nape of my neck...from between my legs.

I curl my fingers around my leather portfolio so hard that I know my knuckles are going white.

"Thank you," I say, and thankfully my voice is as calm and cool as ever. "Can you walk me through what you saw when you pulled up?"

Sutton nods but not before his eyes drop to where my hand clenches around the portfolio. I angle myself away from him ever so slightly so he can't see, and he looks back up. I can't read his gaze...and I'm not sure if I want to.

"I arrived about ninety minutes ago—dispatch sent it out as an alarm call," he starts and then proceeds to give me a clear and concise accounting of his arrival and subsequent search. I'm impressed with his eye for detail—most rookies don't know what to look for on calls like these—and I'm also impressed with the way he describes his search. Brief and without posturing or flourish. Even Frazer couldn't resist the occasional showboating back in his time.

"Thank you," I say when I've finished. "And you're back on duty tomorrow?"

"At three in the afternoon. I'll have my report to you by five."

"Don't make promises you can't keep," Russo advises in a half-supervisory, half-cynical tone, and then she turns to me.

"You'll get it at some point in the next forty-eight."

I make a mental note of that. "Then you're free to go, Officer," I tell him, my eyes dropping one last reluctant time to the hewn, lean length of his body. My little ogle is snagged by the embroidered *J. Sutton* on his uniform shirt.

"Jace," he says softly.

I glance back up at him.

"J is for Jace," he explains.

"Oh," I say and then notice Russo is narrowing her eyes at me. I clear my throat and offer my hand again. "Then thank you, Jace. This has been very helpful."

And I manage not to shiver when he shakes my hand a second time, his eyes falling to my mouth. I also manage not to make a disappointed whimper as his skin parts from mine and he turns to leave.

After he's several paces away, Russo crosses her arms and squints up at the fingernail-shaped moon. "He's only just graduated from field training a few months ago," she says conversationally. "Very young."

"He's very adept," I say in a neutral tone.

"Hmm." She makes the noise in a way that lets me know I'm not fooling her. "Okay, well, I think we're close to being able to release the scene if you're all good?"

"I've got everything I need," I say. "Thanks, Nicki."

She waves me off, reaching down to say something into her radio, and I walk away, trying very hard not to notice the stoic shadow of a certain police officer walking back to his patrol car.

I still notice.

I make a final round through the scene and then walk back to my car, portfolio cradled under my arm. I open it up to where I keep my car key in an inside pocket, and as I'm unlocking the passenger door to set my portfolio in the seat, a patrol car slides into the spot next to me.

The window rolls down, revealing the startlingly handsome profile of Sutton.

"I wanted to make sure you got into your car okay," he says quietly.

I glance around me and then raise an eyebrow. "There are at least seven cops in this lot. And lest you forget, I'm a cop too."

"You don't have your service weapon on you."

"Don't I?" And I'm not exactly sure why I do it, but I can't say my motivation is entirely professional defensiveness. I pull up the hem of my pencil skirt to show where my small Glock is strapped to my inner thigh, revealing my garters and stockings in the process.

I can hear Jace's audible inhale, and when I glance back up at him, his eyes burn with something like fury. But I'm guessing the strain around his mouth and the way he works his jaw to the side has nothing to do with anger.

"It's safer to carry your gun on your hip," he says tightly.

"I don't like to ruin the lines of my skirt," I say. Yes, I'm that vain, although at the first sign of danger, I would have had my weapon out and ready.

I realize I'm still showing off my lingerie when he lets out a low groan. My body responds to his response like he's just touched a match to gasoline, and Russo's voice echoes in my head: *have a little fun.*

Be happy.

It's reckless what I'm about to do. Stupid in ways I'm never stupid in, yet I'm going to do it anyway because I want to. Hell, maybe I *need* to. Maybe my body is so desperate for friction and release that it could have been any man who crossed my path tonight.

But I don't think that's true.

It's something about this too-young-for-me rookie, with his earnest seriousness and intense eyes. With that body that practically thrums with strength.

Every part of it is wrong for a thirty-seven-year-old woman, for a professional, maybe even for an officer of the law, yet I still lean down to his window and say, "Fifty-one thirty-seven Norwood Avenue. The door will be unlocked."

And without waiting for his response, I walk around to the driver's side of my car and leave.

JACE

An hour later I'm in the station, staring at my open locker as if it has answers.

It doesn't.

Fifty-one thirty-seven Norwood Avenue. The door will be unlocked.

My cock, which has been pushing against my zipper since she flashed me that impossibly sexy combination of gun and garter, is hot and throbbing at the idea of going to her house. It's swollen and proud at the pleasure of being picked. My cock wants to go.

Hell, all of me wants to go, if I'm being honest.

Being interviewed by her did nothing to diminish my

slow but growing fascination—a fascination that felt more and more possessive as our conversation went on. The more her aqua eyes flicked over me in that endearingly unchaste way. The hauntingly sexy arch of her eyebrow as she listened. The inadvertent pout of her mouth as she took notes.

The flare of ownership I began to feel was so powerful, so urgent, that I could barely breathe. I didn't care that she was older, that we just met, that while technically permissible, fraternization within rank was still frowned upon.

She was mine.

My ice queen who would thaw only for me.

Except now as I'm changing out, hanging up my duty belt in my locker and lacing up my civvy boots, I'm plagued by questions.

Is this something she does often? Am I not the first young, unattached officer to be picked for this?

Am I imagining her attraction to me? My reaction to her?

And do any of these questions actually matter? It's a spontaneous lay with no promise of more. A single, near-strangerly fuck and then a parting of ways. For all I know, I'll be pushed out the door with a wet dick and one of those small, enigmatic smiles, never to see her again.

I nearly growl at the thought. I don't want a single fuck with Catherine Day. I don't know what I *do* want, but I know this thing stretching and flexing to life inside me won't be satisfied with only tonight.

I'm going to need more.

I'm going to need a lot more.

CHAPTER THREE

CAT

I'm shaking as I walk into my house.

Wild doubts and frenetic surges of panic tumble around inside my mind as I lock up my duty weapon and put my badge and my notes away.

What am I doing? Have I lost my mind?

And will he come?

What if he doesn't?

What if he does?

I pace around the house, turn on some modern cello music, and pour myself a large glass of white wine. It's been three years since I've screwed someone, and even that barely counted because it was the tentative and too-sweet fuck of a successful first date. The man treated me like a china doll—like I'd crack at the first sign of rough handling—and I didn't come. It was rather embarrassing for both of us afterward.

I found excuses to avoid dates after that.

So for three years it's just been me and a small collection of carefully curated toys, and the idea of letting a man back inside my body has me more excited—and more terrified—than I thought possible. What if I've forgotten how to be good at it?

What if it's as disappointing as the last time I invited someone into bed? What if—oh, this is a big one—what if this young man doesn't like my definitely-a-woman-in-her-thirties body?

Worried, I drink more wine and wander back to the front door, debating on whether or not to leave it locked.

Maybe I should. Maybe I should call this entire impulsive, preposterous thing off. I'll leave a note on the door telling him as much and spare us both our pride.

But dammit, I don't want to.

Every time I conjure up an image of Jace Sutton—gray eyes and that young, vigorous body—my own body sizzles with unmet need. And as nervous as I am, I'm certain that if I don't do this, I'll regret it for the rest of my life.

No, I want this. I'm doing it. No matter how embarrassed I'll be in the morning.

I unlock the door.

I'm still dressed, though, and as I finish my wine and set the glass down on the counter, I wonder if I should change that—if I should strip down or don something a bit more overtly sexy. Hell, I'm still in my heels even, still Detective Dry Clean Only.

With a sigh, I decide to change, but as I walk out of my kitchen, I feel it. The distinctive prickle at the back of my neck telling me I'm not alone.

I look up into the window across the breakfast nook and see Jace in the reflection, standing at a careful distance behind me. I'm impressed with how silently he entered my house; I'm not easy to sneak up on.

Even in the reflection—and superimposed over my dark, private backyard—he looks painfully well-built, with the curves of his shoulders and arms pushing at his T-shirt and his jeans showing off his narrow, perfect hips. His chiseled features are still set in that stern, ultraserious expression that I found so compelling earlier, but now there's something else behind that solemnity. Something darker. More primal.

Neither of us says a word, as if we both know that speaking will somehow dilute whatever this is. This assignation. This mystifying attraction between us.

So instead, I give him a steady, almost regal nod, like a queen to her young knight, and he understands immediately, a slow ripple of dangerous lust coursing visibly though him.

He strides forward like a conqueror, and before I can turn to meet him, he has his hand flat between my shoulder blades and he's bending me over the table.

I bend, all the blood in my body pooling in my cunt.

"Jace," I say.

He says nothing in reply but yanks my pencil skirt up to my hips and lets the cool air of the room caress my panty-covered ass. Still silent, his hands find the tops of my stockings and then move to stroke along the lines of my garters. I can't help the moan that escapes me once his fingertips trace up the curve of my ass. Or the second moan when he slides a finger under the edge of my panties and explores the needy kiss of my pussy. He removes the finger and gives me a hard cup, letting me feel the unraveling threads of his control.

Letting me feel how rough he wants to be.

And the ensuing shove and grind of his denim-covered erection against my ass almost feels like an indictment, like he's accusing me of something. I roll my face into the wood surface of the table and shudder.

I like it all way too much.

Have I ever felt like this before? Like a present being unwrapped? Like being both the best and worst thing to happen to a man?

And how does someone so young know to fuck like this?

My panties are torn off—just torn right off my hips without so much as a by-your-leave—and Jace gives my high-heeled foot a vicious kick with his own. It spreads my legs apart, like he's searching me, frisking me, and the thought of that is so wrong and dirty that I whimper into the table.

A long finger makes an approving circle of my now-exposed cunt and then penetrates me in an unhurried but persistent slide. I arch, which earns me another finger and a pleased grunt from him. He gives me a few lazy pumps, paying special attention to the textured spot inside that sends frissons of electric sensation everywhere through my body, but just when I'm starting to get really wet, truly squirmy, he withdraws his hand.

When I look up at the window, I see him staring back at me with darkened, unknowable eyes. He has his fingers in his mouth, and he's sucking my taste right off them.

"Oh God," I whisper. "Oh God."

What have I gotten myself into with him?

A small, barely there quirk of his lips makes me think he can read my thoughts. And the next thing he does is just as carnal, just as vulgar. He unzips his jeans, pulls out his naked cock, and lets it drop right onto the top of my ass. A heavy, marking weight that tells me I wasn't wrong earlier about that superlative bulge in his uniform pants.

Without a word, he extracts a condom from his back pocket and tears it open with his teeth—a move I find animalistically, almost violently, sexual—and then rolls the sheath over his turgid length.

I'm grateful for the condom, really, I am. But at the same time, I almost regret it. I almost wish he'd just penetrate me without one—which is patently nonsensical, as I have no doubt a man like Jace Sutton is fucking his way through the greater Kansas City area. Most cops his age are, which is one of the reasons I've refused to date any of them after Frazer's death.

But Jace has bulldozed past all my usual, prudent precautions. Younger man. Fellow cop. And apparently he's even bulldozed past my common sense about casual sex and protection.

God, I'm fucked in the head.

I can feel the scorching heat of his tip even through the latex as he lazily maps the hollows and folds of my flesh, making everything wet and ready for his invasion.

Then he invades.

The spread of his wide crown into that long-untouched place makes my breath stutter and my fingers curl against the wood, and he's relentless with it, driving in and in and in, tunneling through my tight, squeezing flesh. He pulls back to the crown, and with a hard hand on my hip and a low grunt, he pierces me all the way in.

He stays just like that for a long moment, my body flush against his hips and his free hand smoothing over the strappy bits of garter belt on my bottom and the rucked-up fabric of my skirt. I can't imagine how wanton I look like this, how debauched, my skirt shoved up and my cunt stretched—and all of it without foreplay or an inaugural kiss. Without even a word.

I'm so turned on by it all that I think I'll scream if he doesn't start moving.

I'm shorter than him by a significant amount, even in the steep Manolo Blahniks, and he nudges my feet back together with him still inside in order to get me at the angle he wants. And then he starts to fuck.

Each pull out to the tip is a thrill of friction, and each shove back in is a sear of pressure and heat. He fucks me unapologetically, thoroughly, shoving and driving inward until I can swear the end of his cock is somewhere in my chest, his hands fisting in the expensive fabric of my skirt to bring me back against him harder, faster.

I look up at the window again just to see him—just to see that tall, sturdy body at work—and find him looking at the same thing. Watching us, still clothed, bucking and sweaty. Two cops seeking a desperate, dirty cure for an ancient ache.

His face like this is spellbinding—his dark brows are drawn together in focus and his full mouth is pressed into a solemn line, and he doesn't look like a predator who's caught his prey. He doesn't look like a victorious male who's managed to pin a mate. Not yet. I'm not sure what else he wants until his hand gives my ass a quick *crack* and then just as quickly finds my clit.

Then I know. He wants more from me. He wants me wild. He wants me to come.

I arch, I purr, I twist—his fingers are expert and sure, and they know exactly how to work my flesh, exactly how to circle and press and rub. He watches me carefully in the window, studying my face, and I realize he's learning what I like, gauging my reactions to what he does.

So he sees the frustrated pout when he touches me gently, the ecstatic gasp when he gets rough again and demands a response from my body.

I'm spanked and I let out laughs of surprised pleasure because who knew that could feel so good? So naughty and invigorating, the contrast of the sparkling pain only serving to highlight the pleasure I'm feeling around his thick erection and under his skillful fingers? And there's more, so much more.

My nipples are plucked and rolled through my blouse and bra. My hair is wound in his fist and pulled. My asshole is pressed and played with—with ownership, with male prerogative, as if he has no doubt that he has every right to it.

There's no china doll treatment from Jace Sutton. None at all, and I'm on fire with how much I love it.

My orgasm comes with three years of need roaring behind it—more, *twelve* years of need, twelve years since I've been properly fucked, and even then it still wasn't like this. It still wasn't as dirty or as hard or as fundamental. *This* is how I need to be fucked—how I've always needed to be fucked—and I never knew. I never knew until this one-night stand with a young man I have no right taking to bed.

Bed...kitchen table. Whatever.

With a sobbed moan, I feel the orgasm catch fire around the buried tip of his cock, starting in my belly and yanking at my clit and flickering across every single nerve ending I have. He sucks in a breath as the contractions grip his erection, as if my body is trying to milk the come right up his shaft and into my body, and then he lets loose.

Truly lets loose.

His cock swells bigger and harder than ever, and his hips hammer into the curves of my bottom as if he's trying to wedge his way inside me. I know he wants to come, I know he wants to pump his condom full, and knowing that is enough to set off a second, stronger orgasm inside me.

I let out a soft wail, writhing and kicking my feet as his relentless fucking pins me to the table, and it's too much, it's all too much. I can't handle how viciously my pussy clenches with pleasure. I can't handle the sensory overload of being screwed so ferociously through it all. I wail and I kick, and he grunts and keeps thrusting, and then he lays his upper body over mine, wraps his hand around my throat, and spears me harder than ever, going so deep that I can feel the hair below his navel tickling my ass and the zipper of his jeans biting the tender skin of my thighs.

In near silence he comes, with only a ragged groan on that first exquisite throb to let me know his control is also shaken, and the scalding heat of his seed is palpable even through the latex. His erection flexes and pulses inside me, doing the job it was made for, and I love the feeling of it so much that I tuck my cheek against my shoulder so he can't see the delirious grin on my face.

God, I'd forgotten. Forgotten everything, really, but mostly how good it felt to have someone releasing inside me, filling me with heat as their body jerked in pleasure.

He stays bent over me even after his cock goes still, and he brushes the hair away from my ear so he can ghost his lips over its shell. And for a minute, I think he's going to kiss me. Going to shatter the potent fantasy of this magical encounter with some banal *thank you* or *how was it for you?*

But I underestimate him.

"Don't you ever, *ever*, leave your fucking door unlocked," he whispers against my ear. "Ever fucking again."

Without waiting for a response, he pulls out and steps away, leaving my entire body wet and empty and cold. I hear the clang of the kitchen trash can lid as he throws the condom away, and the purr of his zipper, and then his footsteps to the front door. It opens.

I hear the pointed, deliberate sound of the lock turning and then the door closing behind him.

Jace is gone, having left me bruised and flushed and happy—and safer than how he found me.

And I stay bent over that table for much longer than necessary, smiling into the wood because that unsettled itch from earlier is finally, finally scratched.

CHAPTER FOUR

JACE

I'm edgy as hell as I walk into the station.

I barely slept, could hardly eat this morning, and even the usual grind of weights and cardio at the gym wasn't enough to sharpen my focus. All I could think about was *her*.

Catherine.

Cat.

She was catlike indeed last night, all purrs and sinuous, needy arches. I wonder if she bites. I wonder if she scratches.

I think I might die if I don't find out.

The problem is that I'm not sure I'll have the chance—and even I see the irony of that, because ever since I've come home to Hocker Grove, I haven't exactly been a "find out more" kind of guy.

I left the army, expecting to marry my high school sweetheart, and came home to find that she'd been sweethearting plenty of other guys while I was away. It hurt less than it should have, and I think we'd been nothing more than friends with benefits for a while. But it still made me wary of anything lasting longer than a couple of hours. Once bitten and all that.

Except I want more than a couple of hours with Cat. I want much, much more, and it was only respect for what I thought she needed from our encounter that made me leave. I wasn't going to force myself on her for longer if all she wanted was a nice little fuck to finish off the day.

Not that our fuck was *nice*. Or *little*.

My dick swells as I remember how rough my ice queen wanted it. How she moaned as I pulled her hair and spanked her ass. How fucking sexy and sluttish she looked with that prim skirt over her ass and her pricy garters framing her cunt.

I get to the locker room and lean against my locker, my mind crammed full of last night, my body aching with the memory of it.

What is it about her?

Is it that she's older? Elegant? Mysterious?

Was it the bewitching discovery that if you bent her over a table, all that good breeding disappeared?

I'm not sure. It's all of it combined, maybe. All of it plus seeing her at work last night, so fearless and intelligent and methodical. Knowing her slender, wanton body came paired with steel resolve and a sharp mind.

I'm still chewing over this as I get to roll call and take a chair. Russo goes over the normal beginning of shift stuff—traffic assignments for the afternoon, new slides from vice about a drug ring up north—and then swivels her chair toward me. "Investigations is asking for a uniform to help with the television robberies. I volunteered you."

I'm only half paying attention, my thoughts still fixated on a certain detective. "Pardon?"

"You did a good job last night," Russo says honestly, and it's one of the things I like best about her. She's fair, and while she doesn't effusively praise her squad the way some sergeants do, she consistently recognizes good work. "I was impressed, and Captain Kim in investigations was impressed. We both agree you'd be a good fit to help Day with some of the investigation grunt work."

Hearing her name out loud is like a shot of adrenaline. I sit up straighter, alert. "I'd be working with Detective Day?"

Russo tilts her head at me. "Yeah. That's what I said. That a problem?"

It's the furthest fucking thing in the world from a problem. "No, of course not. Do I need to change shifts?"

"You'll be working whatever they tell you to work," Russo says. "You're temporarily assigned to Day's sergeant and Day's squad. I imagine you'll be working some days, some overnights, that kind of thing. Will that work?"

I have no life outside of this job except for the gym and playing with my niece and nephew. And I'm to the point where I'd happily donate an organ if it meant I could see Day again.

I give Russo an affirmative nod.

"All right. Then get your rookie butt down to investigations and report to Day."

♦♦♦♦

In the history of the HGPD, no one has hauled ass to the investigations station as quickly as I do now, and I test more than a few speed limits as I try to get there before Day clocks out. I park the car and practically jog into the building.

I search out the investigations sergeant for a quick check-in and to verify whom I need to report to for the evening portion of the shift, and then I'm free to find her.

I can admit it now, as I'm stalking through the maze of cubicles to find hers. I can admit how badly I want to fuck her again. How much I hated walking away last night, how my stomach twisted all night long at the thought that she might think badly of me, that she was displeased or unimpressed with what happened.

I want very much for her to be pleased. To be impressed.

I knew all of this earlier, of course, but it's only now as I'm eating up the space between us that I acknowledge the implication.

I want her to be mine.

At least one more time.

Cat's cubicle is tucked away in a far corner, and it's larger than most. A subtle indication of her position in the unit. A little digging this morning while Romero and I were at the station gym netted me the information that Cat is the lead persons detective and usually takes point on the city's homicides, when we have them—which is rarely—working assaults, batteries, and stalking the rest of the time.

She has the highest case clearance rate of any other detective in her unit and has for years. She did a stint with the KBI—HGPD loaned her out for that one—and frequently gets called in by other agencies to help with difficult cases. The "frigid bitch" Quinn was talking about is possibly the best cop in the department—and manages to be the best without fanfare or arrogance.

And she surrendered all that intelligence and discipline into my hands last night. The significance of that is potent. Intoxicating.

Russo made it sound as if Captain Kim had decided to put me on the burglary case, but I can't help but hope that Day asked for me. That she liked my performance—both at the scene and in her kitchen—enough to trust me with her presence again. I want her to trust me. I want it as directly and forcefully as I've wanted anything else that matters.

And now I'm thinking about wanting her in the noisy, fluorescent bullpen.

Get it under control, Sutton.

I'm always professional and respectfully subordinate—a gift from the army days—but even walking up to her cubicle has my cock thick and my blood hot. My heart is in my throat like I'm a teenage boy about to ask a girl to his first dance, and I'm itching just to *see* her, just to be *close* to her.

Except when I get to her, she's not alone.

A man, probably just on the young side of forty, is standing in the cubicle opening with an elbow propped on the chest-high wall and one dress-shoed foot crossed behind the other. He's in a tailored blue suit, the kind that costs as much as I make in a month, and it showcases an impressively fit body. There's no wedding ring on his hand, and he's leaning in to talk to Cat in a familiar manner that makes me want to smash something.

When I get to the cubicle entry myself, I see Cat sitting in her chair, looking radiant in that tasteful way of hers and laughing at something he's said.

I hate him immediately.

Her eyes slide over to me and widen, and for a moment, I see desire flash in those sparkling depths—but as soon as I see it, it's gone, and she's the aloof queen once more.

"Sutton," she says calmly. "What brings you to this station?"

Ah, so she didn't know I was coming. Which means she didn't ask for me.

Shit.

Pushing down my disappointment, I reply, "Russo's lending me out to you. It's gone through Kim and everything, so...I'm at your disposal. Starting now."

I feel a rush of male satisfaction as my subtext sends pink blooming along her cheekbones.

"How nice," she murmurs, her sea-colored eyes dropping down to her shoes. She takes a breath, and when she looks back up at me, she seems to have control of herself again. "Sutton, have you met our new assistant district attorney, Kenneth Goddard? He used to be one of the best defense lawyers in town before he moved away a few years ago, but now he's back and fighting for the side of good." She gives him a quick, teasing grin with her last statement, and I hate him even more.

Kenneth laughs. "Good is subjective. You know that."

She makes a face. "Maybe in criminal defense, but you were getting doctors and rich kids out of DUIs, Ken. Not exactly a hero's fare."

"But you admit I *was* good at it." He grins and then turns to me, extending a hand. He's good-looking, damn him, in a WASPy way. Medium height, dark-blond hair, and a fucking cleft in his chin. His fine-boned face and expensive haircut make me think he's known wealth long before defending assholes for lots of money.

"Nice to meet you, Officer Sutton," Kenneth says easily. It takes every ounce of self-control I have to shake his hand.

"Likewise," I lie.

Cat stands up, smoothing down her skirt as she does. It's another pencil skirt, dark gray this time, and I nearly need to excuse myself after thinking about how good it would look shoved up to her waist.

She seems to have the same thought, because her hands shake as she smooths the fabric again and she can't look me in the face.

"Kenneth is the ADA who will handle most of the medium-level persons crimes moving forward, so he was just in to talk to Kim."

"Well, and to catch up with you, Cat," Kenneth interjects.

He calls her Cat. I don't fucking like that. Not at all.

And I like it even less when he catches her hand and gives it a quick squeeze. Jealousy flares through me so hot and fast that I think I might erupt, because how dare he touch her in front of me?

Stop it, my conscience warns. *She's not yours.*

For her part, Cat seems as surprised by the hand squeeze as I'm not. Any idiot can tell that this Kenneth is interested in her, that he wants her. It's all over his body language, in the gaze that can't stop dropping to her tits and tracing the subtle curve her pussy makes against her tight skirt.

He wants her, and worse—I think there's some history here. When he lets go of her hand, it's with the satisfaction of someone reclaiming lost territory.

"I hope you don't mind if I give you a call?" he asks, touching her elbow. I nearly deck him.

Her eyes dart to me, her mouth pursed in a moue that I'm beginning to recognize as her thinking face. "I suppose that would be okay," she says hesitantly, and something inside me dies a little.

It's impossible not to notice how good they look together. Not to notice he's got the same elegant, well-bred features she does. The same expensive taste in clothes. They're the same age and have the same precision of speech and bearing.

Compared to him, I feel young and dumb. A blunt, inexperienced instrument. A big, strong body to ride and then forget about the next day.

I take a step back as he gives her a winning smile and then turns that smile on me. I don't think I'm imagining the glint of victory in his stare as he holds out a hand for me to shake again. Nor the trace of smugness in his voice when he says, "Officer Sutton."

I shake his hand, letting my nod be my only response.

"I'll talk to you later, Cat," he says, the words laden with meaning, and then he leaves.

And I'm not sure what I feel, except jealous and possessive and maybe the tiniest bit insecure. Especially looking at Cat, now leaning over her desk to get her portfolio, her pale-blond hair swinging in soft, coiffed waves, one delicate high heel kicked back for balance.

She looks like perfection. Like the kind of woman who should be with a hotshot lawyer, pampered and taken to restaurants I've never even heard of—and wouldn't be able to pronounce their names even if I had. Kenneth is the right kind of man for her. Not me.

But I don't think I care.

I don't care because I may not be rich, but I've known rich men and I know how they think. I know exactly how Kenneth sees Cat. She's a shiny, beautiful thing to him, like a sleek sports car glinting in the lot, and once he acquires her, he'll want her off the streets. He'll want her sitting at home, safe and gathering dust, until he sees fit to take her out and show her off.

I don't care because even though I barely know her, I can see a life like that would make her miserable. She can't be fettered down to play house, leaving only to be gala arm candy. She needs to be handled according to her strength—used and adored in equal measure—and she needs someone who doesn't want to change a single fucking thing about her. Not her job or her drive or anything.

And I don't care because I felt her body against mine last night. I heard her fingernails against the wood and her soft, euphoric moans as she came over and over again. I saw her quiver as I spanked her and pulled her hair. I felt her get wetter and wetter as I kicked her legs apart and played with her asshole.

There's no way in hell Kenneth would be able to give her what she needs.

And I can.

Maybe it's as simple as that.

But as Cat straightens up, gives me one of those thoughtful half pouts, and says, "Okay, Sutton, what am

I going to do with you?" I worry that it's not going to be simple at all.

CHAPTER FIVE

CAT

The sight of Jace standing in front of me stunned me so much that I don't know how I fumbled my way through the rest of the conversation with Kenneth. There I was, praying Kenneth couldn't tell how gingerly I was sitting on my office chair because I'd been reamed to heaven and back by a gorgeous man who'd been a baby while I was in high school, and then Jace just *appeared,* as if my tender cunt had summoned him into existence.

The difference between Jace and Kenneth was beyond startling. Next to the raw, potent presence of Jace in uniform, Kenneth looked like a photocopy of a Brooks Brothers ad. Where Jace was hard and lean from PT in the desert, Kenneth had the sort of self-conscious physique that came from paying a trainer a lot of money. And where Jace's almost-rugged features are pulled into a look of stern detachment, Kenneth was all genteel symmetry and practiced smiles.

I've never felt that Kenneth was *unattractive* before now, but with Jace next to him...Jace might as well have been the only man on earth as far as my body was concerned. The sheer power radiating from his wide shoulders and crossed arms and wide, booted stance was enough to make me embarrassingly, shamefully wet. I stood up before I left a damp spot on my skirt.

"Okay, Sutton, what am I going to do with you?" I glance down the bullpen, relieved to see that no one is watching the Ice Queen blush over a rookie, and then I glance toward the door as I think. I have a few follow-ups I need to do, and I could probably task some of those to Jace, but if I'm honest, I'm not ready for us to part ways just yet. It feels like some kind of bizarre gift from the universe that he's here at all. One of those coincidences that I'm in danger of making too much of, when I should just be grateful for the extra help. Especially when that help is as capable and competent as Jace Sutton.

The thought grounds me in the here and now. Back to reality and the case. With a deep breath, I turn to him and force myself to be nothing more than professional. At least in my words, if I can't be in my thoughts.

"I think it's best if we go through the evidence together, make sure you know everything I do," I say. "Kim's given me the meeting room across the hall as a base camp, so let's start there."

I gesture to the meeting room in question, but Jace doesn't look where I indicate. Instead, he gives me a slow, heated once-over that makes my belly clench.

"I'm happy to start wherever you are," he says after a minute, with just the barest hint of an eyebrow raise to underscore that he's not only talking about the case, and then he turns and walks to the meeting room with the confident stride of a man who's been to war.

It's that presence that seals the deal, I decide as I follow him out of the little hallway made by my cubicle and the meeting room. With his kissable lips and long eyelashes, he could easily be too handsome to be powerful, but there's something about those stormy gray eyes and the low voice and the authority he exudes simply by standing in place. It's what makes him look like a cop and not like an actor who plays a cop on TV.

He opens the door to the meeting room and flicks on the light, and I can't help it. I really can't. It's these fucking uniform pants and how they display the molded, muscled curve of his ass.

I look.

I *gawk*. Like a schoolgirl after the cute boy, I gawk.

And then I remember I'm thirteen years older than him and my gawking probably looks more like a leer.

Stop it, Cat. This can't happen.

There's a million reasons I can't fuck Jace Sutton again. In our department, officers and detectives share the same rank, and fraternization is allowed within rank, but it's still wildly unprofessional...even more so now that he's been assigned to my case.

And then there's the age difference. A twenty-four-year-old cop with a giant cock and flat abs? I have no doubt there's a bevy of badge bunnies with limber, nubile bodies waiting to crawl into his lap face first and that he probably went home so fast after fucking me because he had no desire to fuck me again. Why would he want to fuck an old lady when there's probably an infinite supply of eager twenty-somethings waiting to fall into his bed?

The thought is depressing.

But I'm not in the habit of allowing myself self-pity and never have been, even after Frazer's death. I enjoyed last night, and I refuse to regret it. Even if it's time to get back to real life now.

And I'm all ready for real life, for the contained control I normally enjoy, just as soon as I'm done looking at Sutton's ass. Which I am. I definitely am done looking—okay, maybe just one more peek—

Jace turns faster than I anticipate, and there can be no doubt he catches me looking. His usual brooding scowl gets scowlier.

Which is fair. There's no doubt it's improper to be caught ogling your young coworker's ass, even if you did fuck him the night before. But I can't pretend shame. I can't pretend there isn't a tiny part of me that feels entitled to look.

I tilt my head and allow him a little smile. *You caught me.*

He kicks the door shut, and in a heartbeat I'm pushed against the wall and trapped between his hands planted on either side of my head as my phone and portfolio tumble to the floor.

I'm caged in by two hundred pounds of angry male muscle, but I haven't been afraid of big, grumpy cops since I started academy—and anyway, my body associates all this intensity and closeness from Jace with something close to danger but much, much more fun.

"You're looking at me like you want to be bent over a table again," he says in a silky voice.

"Maybe."

He glances down at my nipples, erect and making

themselves known against the thin fabric of my blouse.

"Is that for me?"

"Who else would it be for?"

"Kenneth."

I make a dismissive noise, and my cop narrows his eyes.

"He wants to fuck you," he growls. "I don't like it."

I lift an eyebrow. "I don't see how that's any of your business."

More scowling. "Still. He's an asshole."

It's so churlish, so very male, that I have to laugh a little, and his gaze snags on my smiling mouth and goes from angry to something different. Something greedy.

"He's not an asshole," I say. "He's very nice. Even if he were an asshole, however, it still wouldn't be any of your business."

"You've fucked him," the sulky rookie says. "Haven't you?"

There's no point in lying, not when Jace and I are as little to each other as Kenneth and I are. Or at least as little as Jace and I *should* be to each other. "Three years ago. One date. He ended up moving right after to be closer to his kids, and that was the end of it."

"Except he's back now," Jace points out. "And he wants to pick up where you left off."

"I'm reiterating again that this is none of your business."

Not that Jace is wrong. I think Kenneth would very much like to pick up where we left off. Have more china doll sex. And in the three years since he left, I've thought about it. Thought about how long the nights are getting, how my house seems to feel emptier and emptier and emptier. I never cared too much about becoming a spinster—I've even railed against the label as patriarchal bullshit—but though I don't feel desperate to marry or start a family, I do feel...lonely.

And wouldn't Kenneth be an easy solution? He already has two lovely daughters, so if we had children, it would be because we wanted them, not because we felt middle age bearing down on us. And we run in the same circles, share many of the same friends. It makes sense.

In contrast, Jace makes no sense. He's the opposite of the pro-Kenneth list. Too young to settle down, and I bet too wild too. Just like Frazer at that age, working hard, playing hard—drinks and girls and danger. There's no easy security in Jace, no clear path to a future.

So why am I uninterested in Kenneth?

And why am I so inexorably drawn to this young cop instead?

I look up into Jace's stern face. "Why do you care?"

It's the wrong thing to say. It betrays too much of my own conflicted desires, and Jace, like any good predator, smells my weakness.

"Do you want me to care?" he asks, his voice turning low and rough.

He's visibly shaking with restraint now, his hands balled into fists on either side of me, his pulse thrumming fast in his neck. Every long, diamond-cut inch of his body is desperate to press against mine; I don't have to look down to know he's hard. His jaw is tense, rigid, a small muscle jumping along it. He looks like he wants to fuck me right through the wall.

God, this is sexy. It's all so fucking sexy...

My composure is gone. My control is shot. There's only

him, smelling like leather and the barest hint of tea tree oil. Rugged and clean. I lean forward and run my nose along the edge of his jaw to smell it better.

He freezes.

His jaw is clean-shaven, but that five o'clock shadow is beginning to make itself known—just a hint of raspiness over his warm, sculpted jaw. It tickles against my nose, and his scent is even stronger like this. If the Yankee Candle store sold a candle that smelled like Jace, women would stop going on dates altogether.

"Cat," he rumbles in warning.

This growling version of Jace is going to be the death of my panties. I rub my chest against his hard, body-armored one and smile into his neck.

He lets out a long breath. A "now I see" breath.

"Do you like me being jealous of him?" His hand drops from beside my head and slowly, deliberately palms my cunt through my skirt. "Do you like it when I'm possessive?"

My head drops back against the wall as my hips push against his touch. Pleasure curls, dark and smoky, through my belly and chest, and I know the answer before I admit it aloud. "Yes."

"I know you do." He says it matter-of-factly, in this almost-arrogant way that leaves no room for doubt.

I do like it. He did know.

It's that straightforward.

He reaches over with his free hand and locks the meeting room door, and for the first time, I appreciate how isolated it is. Near nothing else except my cubicle, with no internal windows or shared doors. And when Jace flicks off the light, leaving only the afternoon sunlight straining against the metal blinds of the exterior windows, I know we're essentially hidden here. As long as we stay silent, no one will know.

Ohhhh, this is such a bad idea. But it doesn't stop me from rocking my cunt against Jace's peremptory touch.

"Tell me," he says, leaning close and ghosting his mouth over my jaw. "Did he fuck you right? Did he make that little pussy of yours happy?"

My eyelids flutter at his dirty words, even as the sensible part of my mind rears up to scream *it's none of your business!* I shouldn't betray poor Kenneth's ego this way. I shouldn't. But then Jace presses hard enough to make me moan, and I think maybe I don't care and that I'll tell him anything to keep this jealous, ravenous side of him around.

"Did he?" he demands again, impatient with my silence, curling his fingers to catch my clit with more pressure.

"No," I relent in a whimper. "No, he didn't."

Jace nods to himself, as if confirming knowledge he already had. "He was too gentle, wasn't he? Tried to fuck you easy and sweet?"

His fingers are now at the hem of my skirt, dragging it up to my waist. I'm squirming to get his touch back where I need it, back where I'm wet and aching, back where only he can soothe me.

"Too bad he didn't know there isn't anything easy about you," Jace says, one hand pushing my panties aside and the other hand fisting in my hair. He makes me watch as he pushes his fingers inside me and fucks me with them. "Too bad he didn't know you're the furthest thing from *sweet*."

"Then what am I?" I dare him, as if any dare has teeth when you're fucking yourself on someone's hand.

But Jace responds immediately, his nostrils flaring and his eyes blazing bright. "You're *mine*," he seethes and yanks me in for a brutal kiss.

Our lips meet, hot and urgent, and then his tongue seeks out the seam of my mouth, demanding entry, demanding succor. I let him in. I let him taste my mouth for the first time as he finger-fucks me against the wall and fists my hair. He sweeps through my mouth the way he does everything—quietly, intensely, and with raw, male power. But I manage to break his silence and elicit a long groan from him when I kiss him back, when I stroke my tongue along his the way I would his cock, with flickers and swirls and promise.

I shouldn't do this. Fraternization is fine, but sex on duty definitely isn't—and we're not only on duty but also on police department property. In the same building as twenty other cops. I should push Jace away, straighten up my skirt, and act like Catherine Day again.

I'm tired of acting like Catherine Day. The thought adds to the restless itch that's been crawling through my blood since I saw Jace standing firm and sure next to my cubicle. I'm tired of being lonely, of being the best, of being the sort of woman that would fit a man like Kenneth.

And as foolish as it is, something about Jace drives back this lonely ache and makes me feel alive again—and I can't surrender that to the faceless pestle of propriety and professionalism. Not yet, anyway.

I reach up and grab his collar. "I want to get fucked again," I say against his mouth.

He doesn't flinch. Doesn't hesitate.

"Here?" he asks.

"Here."

His mouth comes back over mine, hard, as he adds another finger inside me. "I don't have a condom, Cat."

My high heels make it difficult to rise and press to get the friction I want, and Jace knows it, using my inability to move to tease me, to edge me along the brink until I think I might go mad.

"I don't care," I pant. "I'm using birth control. I'm clean. Fuck me bare."

He pulls back enough to catch my eyes, and the raw lust there is enough to make my knees buckle. "Cat."

"Are you clean, Jace? Say you are. Say you'll stick that beautiful cock inside me. Say you'll do it now."

"I'm clean."

I nearly faint in relief.

"If I do this, I'm going to come inside you," he warns. His fingers stroke inside my cunt to underscore his words. "Going to make that pussy mine. Got it?"

"Oh God, yes, please, please do that." I'm dangerously close to babbling now, my hands still twisting in his collar.

He gives me a nod. "And you have to be quiet," he says, his free hand unbuckling his duty belt. "Can you do that?"

"I'd like to promise that I can?" I offer, and for the first time in our acquaintance, I see his mouth hitch up in a smile. It kicks the breath right out of my lungs, he's so handsome.

He slides his fingers free and says, "Open." And then my mouth is filled with his fingers—which taste like me. It's so filthy, I can't stand it.

"Keep your legs spread for my cock," he rumbles, and I obey.

CHAPTER SIX

JACE

I'm about to fuck Catherine Day in the investigations station.

More than that, I'm about to fuck her surrounded by boxes of evidence for the case we should be working on, with my new supervisor down the hallway, in broad fucking daylight, and I don't care.

In my defense, I didn't stand a damn chance after she murmured those magic words.

I want to get fucked again.

Although it's possible I didn't ever stand a chance. Not after catching her staring at my ass in that obscene way of hers. Not after seeing her beautiful and polished, sitting in her cubicle. Maybe not even after last night.

One hit and I'm a goner. Cat Day: gateway drug. Except she's a gateway drug to more of her. She's got me craving and trembling for just one more taste. Just one more touch.

Running me extra ragged is the slow unraveling of her own self-control—all that equilibrium and poise vanishing under my lips, my fingers. Seeing my scent drive her wild, feeling my jealousy get her wet. Her plea for us to fuck bare.

There's a good reason I don't pack condoms in my badge

wallet or uniform pockets, and it's because it's against policy to fuck on duty. And when I say *against policy*, I mean I'll be outside on my ass so fast I won't even have time to put on my sunglasses.

But I don't even care right now, because right now? With my fingers in Cat's mouth and her eyes burning aqua against mine?

It would be worth it.

It only takes one hand to unbuckle the duty belt and only a moment to pop off the keepers and drop it to the ground. I don't bother pulling the underbelt free—I unfasten it to expose my pants button, and then I'm able to unzip.

Cat makes a noise around my fingers—a sort of whine that communicates one thing: *hurry*.

My cock is so eager to be free that it nearly slaps up against my abs after I tug down the waistband of my boxers. And I can already feel the cool kiss of air along my tip, telling me I have pre-come beading there. After that, it's just some pragmatic rearranging of fabric to make sure my cock is unimpeded and her panties are shoved well free.

"Shh," I tell her and remove my fingers from her mouth. I need both hands to do this: a hand for grabbing one stocking-covered thigh to hike to my hip and the other to stir my head around her opening.

But she can't *shh*, at least not very well. The minute the hot, taut skin of my crown kisses along her pussy, she lets out a noise that has me ready to blow—and would also let anyone walking by know what we are doing.

A quick time-out then. I drop her leg, and amid a whine of

protest at the lack of contact between us, I unclip her garters and pull down and remove her panties.

And then I put them in her mouth.

Not a lot—not enough to truly gag her or make her uncomfortable—but enough that she has to work to keep them in place. Enough that she'll be reminded to stay silent, because we can't get caught.

Not only do I not want to get fired, but if I manage to get one of the best detectives in the metro fired because I couldn't keep it in my pants? I'm never going to not hate myself.

So it's panties and silence for now.

Her eyes are wide and wondering on mine as I trace a finger around her perfect mouth. The lace spilling out of it only highlights the smoothness of her lips, the natural, lipstick-free pink of them.

"That's better," I say quietly. "Can't have you getting caught, can we? Can't have you trying to explain why you needed my cock so badly you couldn't wait."

She closes her eyes and nods, and I use the moment to bring her leg back to my hip again. With her opened up and her mouth full, I can now freely nudge at the entrance waiting for me without worrying about her pleasured noises bringing the entire investigations unit running in.

She's hot and slick, and shudders race up and down my spine as I find the little opening all tucked away in her wet folds and forge in. I've never felt this—*never*—not even as a dumbass teenager or when I thought I was going to marry Brittany. Never had my bare cock surrounded by a hot pussy, skin to skin, with nothing in between. It's impossible to describe, impossible even to process, and I make an unholy grunt as I finally reach home.

Cat makes a noise around her panties, and I look into her wide, surprised eyes. She looks down at where we're joined, past my rucked-up uniform shirt and her crumpled skirt to where only a glimpse of my thick shaft is visible before it disappears inside her.

She makes the noise again, and I realize she's saying *oh*.

Yeah. *Oh.*

"Shit, Cat," I whisper, feeling undone, vulnerable with the sheer experience of taking her like this. "How the fuck did I walk away from you last night?"

I emphasize my point with a thrust, testing the angle and the pressure of us like this. "How did I not stay and fuck and fuck and fuck until neither of us could walk?"

Her eyes flutter closed in that way I'm learning means she's aroused beyond belief, and I reward her with another slide—this one with a little grind against her clit at the end. Her supporting leg nearly buckles, and she grabs on to my shoulders for balance, her manicured fingernails digging in through my shirt as I start truly pounding into her.

Even in her sexy-as-fuck heels, the mismatch in our heights make the angle a little rough, a little desperate. I have to bend my knees and palm her ass to hitch her higher against me, and she finally wraps her other leg around my waist and locks her heels at the small of my back, now fully pinned against the wall by my cock and the force of our need.

It's grinding and wet and messy. She clings to me, carrying most of her weight with her clenched thighs and her arms braced on my shoulders, but I have to keep her pressed against the wall for balance. Which keeps the swollen bead of her clit tight against me, keeps it rubbed and squeezed and all the good stuff that makes her writhe and quake and pant around the lace in her mouth.

It's the lace I watch as I fuck her, focusing on the delicate clovers and whorls of the fabric. On the glimpses of full pink lips underneath, of pinker tongue and white teeth. At first, I do it to distract myself from the insane feeling of her pussy around my cock and that shapely ass cradled in my palms, but then it becomes its own torture. Her perfect mouth, tempting in its lush elegance, crammed full of my homemade gag. And she let me—she just *let me*—as if I had every right to gag her. Every right to do whatever I want.

I curl in, snag her earlobe with my teeth. "Get there, Cat," I grate out. "You feel too good, and you have to get there because I can't last."

She nods, and the movement brushes her panties across my polyester uniform shirt with a gentle rasp that drives me wild. I have to close my eyes and conjure up memories of crawling through frozen mud at boot camp and eating rubbery DFAC food to stave off the knot of orgasm that's currently pulling tight at the base of my cock. I can't come yet...I can't come yet...her first...*I can't come yet*—

Cat manages to find a new way to bear down onto me that gives her clit even more attention. We're toiling hard, the both of us, sweat misting damp across our skin and breathing fast, short, feverish breaths, and I see the moment our labor pays off. The moment she finally catches hold of her release, and with a whimper, she drops her head onto my shoulder and quivers around my cock. Big, rolling quivers that clench down at the tip of me buried somewhere deep inside her.

She's mumbling something around her panties as she rides out her orgasm, the same thing over and over again, and it takes me a few times hearing it to realize it's my name. It's my fucking name.

Jace jace jace oh god jace—

My orgasm slams into me so hard that I want to roar with the sheer ecstasy of it, the primal victory of pumping my come deep into a woman and giving her everything I have, every last fucking drop.

It's messy, so much messier than usual, and as I keep fucking her through the hot slick of my own seed, I remember that it's because there's no condom to keep our bodies separate, no barrier to contain the biological result of thrusting, pumping pleasure.

It's just my come and the wet evidence of her orgasm, mixing hot and perfect around us, and feeling it drives my climax on and on and on. I ejaculate with brutal, seemingly never ending throbs, each pulse like a jolt of pure heaven sizzling straight through me, and for a moment, I feel more naked than my still-clothed situation should permit. Like Cat can see more than just my face or my bare cock but something inside me. Like she can see me in a way no one ever has before.

It freaks me the fuck out—but maybe not as much as it should.

Maybe I want her to see me because I want *her*. Period. Everything about her I want, and I want more of it, and I want more of it for a long time.

When I set her carefully on her feet and slide out, come drips out of her, and one slow drop lands on the toe of her red high heel.

"Jesus fucking Christ, I might need to come again," I say as I watch it happen.

Cat just gives a little croon in response, yanks out her makeshift gag, and then uses the panties to clean off the inside of her thighs.

I groan again. "Fuck, now I really need to."

She looks up with some amusement and then back down at my cock, which is already stiffening, ready for round two.

"*Young* man," she purrs.

I have no doubt she could keep up with me, though, given the way she's biting her lip and eyeing my erection right now. If we were at her place or mine—if we were anywhere else—we could go as many rounds as we needed to scratch the itch. As it is, I'm almost considering asking her for another—just one more, just real fast—because I'm not satisfied, not satisfied at all.

She's still all rumpled and flushed, and that pussy is still exposed and taunting me with its silky blond curls and swollen, florid petals, and I just need one more time, one more fuck. Then I can start thinking straight again.

Cat's cell phone rings from the floor where she dropped it earlier, and as she bends down to get it, I hear a voice from outside the door. Two voices.

Shit.

The look of alarm I shoot Cat is reflected right back at me, and she ignores the phone in favor of setting herself to rights as quickly as possible. She doesn't bother fastening her garter—simply yanks down her skirt, smooths her shirt, and digs in her portfolio for a small elastic hair tie. She pulls her mussed hair into a ponytail as I zip up and manage to get my duty belt on with some degree of quietude, although the keepers I have to shove into my pockets because I don't have enough time to fasten them on. I shove her panties in my pocket too, unlock the door, and flick on the light.

Within seconds of us getting seated at the table, there's a casual knock and then the door pops open.

"Hey," Sergeant Hougland says. The door opens more, and he's with—aw, fuck—he's with Captain Kim.

I see Cat swallow in the corner of my vision.

But both administrators seem unsuspecting and oblivious as they come in, and they don't seem to pick up on Cat's pink cheeks or the smell of sex in the room.

Not that I can relax any. I just had delicious, wet, unprotected sex in a police station. Sex that is still all over my skin and probably my clothes too, and now my new supervisors are strolling in for a chat. I hold myself as rigid and as detached as I can manage, hoping it's not obvious that I was a rutting, eager beast just a few minutes ago.

"Day, we're just swinging by on our way out to a meeting to see if you got that report I sent over from KCPD."

Cat nods, folding her hands over her crossed legs, looking every bit the untouchable ice queen she's rumored to be. Except between those crossed legs is a cunt that's currently leaving a wet spot on that dry-clean-only skirt.

I feel a jerk of primitive satisfaction at the thought.

"I did," she says crisply. "It was a report full of nothing, which I expected."

"No leads on their end?"

"No leads," she affirms. "Same as what KCKPD and the other Johnson County agencies said. The televisions aren't being sold in the area, if they're being sold at all. It's like they're being stolen and hoarded."

"That's not the usual way of things." Hougland sighs, as if personally put out that these criminals aren't following the template. "You think they're planning on selling them in one big shipment?"

"It would be foolish," Cat says and lifts a shoulder in a graceful shrug. "But I suppose we can't rule anything out. I'm pulling together a list of plates that have hit plate readers mounted on traffic lights near the burglarized offices. Any duplicate hits—especially in the hours before and after the burglary—I'm going to follow up on. I suppose a next step could be seeing if any of those car owners have made payments for a storage unit in the metro. We might find our televisions there."

Hougland and Kim are nodding. "When it's warrant time, loop me in," Hougland says. "I want to look it over before we submit it to a judge."

"Of course," Cat says coolly, and then Kim and Hougland ramble on a bit more about this and that before one of them glances at the clock on the wall and gives a theatrical sigh.

"It's time to head out. Great work, Catherine," Kim says, and they finally leave.

When the door closes, I look across the table at Cat and

see a peculiar tightness around her mouth. If I had to guess, I'd say she looks pissed, but on Cat, it's hard to guess at any emotion because she's constantly wearing this forbidding, almost haughty shell.

"Hougland tick you off?" I hazard.

She looks back at me with some surprise and then gives a reluctant, sly grin. "That obvious, huh?"

"Nothing about you is obvious," I say, and I mean it. "But I'm determined to learn every single thing about you. Including how you feel and what you hide."

Her lips part, ever so slightly, and she shakes her head. "I keep thinking I know the box to put you in, and then you keep surprising me..."

I'm dying to know what box she wants to put me in, but she continues.

"Yes, Hougland has been frustrating to deal with. He just transferred into investigations last month, after I'd been put on the robberies. He's old and a man, and he has old-man ideas about what I'm capable of. He's been micromanaging the hell out of this case, and me, and I don't deserve that."

I love how unapologetically she talks about this. How fearlessly she calls out Hougland on his bullshit.

I don't know what she sees in my face just now, but she raises an eyebrow. "I have pride too, you know," she says. "Cop pride is not exclusive to people with penises."

"That's not what I was thinking."

"What *were* you thinking?"

"That I'd like to have a few rounds in the ring with Hougland until he started treating you with respect."

This seems to please her—fine little lines bracket the corners of her full mouth and spread out from her eyes. "*Young* man," she says again, but this time she says it with fondness. With affection.

I don't realize how long our gazes are locked in this sort of baffled, lustful fascination with each other until she clears her throat and looks down.

"Jace, about today," she begins, and my stomach sinks. I know that tone of voice. I know it because I'm usually the one to use it. Usually the one to tell someone I just fucked that it's been a great time and now I'll get them an Uber.

I don't help her along with this because I don't want it. I know I almost got her fired just now by screwing her in her own police station. I know this is nuts, but dammit—I don't care.

"You know what I'm going to say," she says tactfully, gently. "I am...rather charmed by you, but I think you also charm me out of all reason. And it doesn't make sense anyway."

"What doesn't make sense?" I genuinely don't understand. I find her wildly sexy, wildly intelligent, and I want to fuck her every chance I get from now until...well, I don't know until when, but for a good long time. What else does there need to be?

Her eyelashes sweep down in a dark fan over her cheeks as she chooses her words carefully. "Me and another cop. I haven't dated another cop since Frazer, and I shouldn't start now."

"Why?" The word is out of my mouth before I can really process that she just brought up her dead fiancé and that I should proceed with diplomacy.

She's still looking down as she thinks. "What happened when he died—I can't live through that again. I barely survived it the first time." She meets my gaze again, and I'm nearly rocked back by the emotion simmering in her blue-green eyes. "I know what they say about me. That I'm incapable of grief or love or any feeling at all. The Ice Queen. The truth is I wanted to die with Frazer that night, and a part of me did. And what's left won't survive if it happens again."

"So no cops...because they might die? Hate to tell you this, Cat, but everyone dies. In every profession."

She presses her lips together. "It's not the same. And cops are reckless, risky, and rough. They get hard. Now that I'm older and know that, I don't know if it's what I want in my future."

"I didn't hear any complaints about my getting hard earlier."

She looks like she wants to roll her eyes. "And you're young, Jace. Inappropriately young."

"I don't mind," I tell her. "The difference in our ages doesn't bother me at all."

She looks away. "It will."

"Why?"

She still won't look at me. "Because you're young and sexy and you'll have equally young and sexy girls raining from the sky. You deserve better than wasting your time on me." She stands up to leave.

I stand up too, not willing to let this go. "Cat—"

She holds up a hand. "It's enough, Jace. It's enough to make it a bad idea. I'm thirteen years older, and you're the kind of man I've sworn to stay away from anyway. Maybe you can fuck the same person over and over again without feelings getting involved, but I look at you and I know that's not going to be possible for me." She takes a deep breath and meets my eyes. "I look at you and I think you might be capable of breaking my heart."

And with that bombshell, she crosses to the door without so much as a *goodbye* and leaves me alone in the meeting room. The room that still smells like us.

CHAPTER SEVEN

CAT

It's quite frigid between us after that.

Perhaps the frigidity is all on my side. Perhaps I'm the one making it cold, because more than once this week, I've caught him staring at me with a heated need that nearly made my skin catch fire.

He still wants me. And fuck all if I don't still want him.

But life isn't that easy, and after the close call of Kim and Hougland nearly walking in on us, I'm reminded of what matters most.

Working. The. Damn. Case.

So we work the case. Jace has officially switched to day shift now, so I actually do get him up to speed on everything. I assign him to some follow-ups and calls to witnesses to verify reports, and we manage to get through it without any unprofessional interaction. Or, you know, more police station intercourse.

I can't stop aching for him, though. Those intense gray eyes that get darker and stormier when they look at me. That frowning mouth that I now know can be kissed into softness. Those big, rough hands that handle my body the way I've always needed to be handled, even if I hadn't known it. More than once when we're working in the meeting room, I excuse myself to use the restroom and then rub myself to a quick, urgent orgasm in the stall just to take the edge off. It's the only time I've ever been grateful for the gender disparity in the police force—more privacy in the bathroom to indulge this unseemly need for a much-younger-than-me man.

It's a long week, with both of us unhappy and strained and physically uncomfortable. And the week gets even longer when I realize I have my low-light range recertification waiting for me at the end of it. It's the annual test I have to take to prove to my department I can operate a firearm in the dark. But I know I can operate a firearm in the dark and operate it well.

It was how I killed Frazer's murderer all those years ago.

And therein lies the problem. It's the one thing I do each year that brings it all back. The dark, shitty house in the worst part of town. The frantic babbles of the meth addict who'd just stabbed Frazer and left him to bleed out on the dirty floor. The kick of the gun in my hand as I fired and the killer fell. Trying to save the man I was supposed to marry...

My hands shake as I pull my vest over my shirt. I opted out of my usual uniform of silk and tailored skirts today, knowing I'd be striding and darting around the darkened range rooms. I'm wearing the blue, like a real cop. Something I rarely do since I transferred to investigations after Frazer's death, leaving the world of uniforms and midnight stabbings behind.

So here I am—polyester uniform shirt, utility pants, load-bearing vest. I'm even wearing boots instead of my customary heels. I have to force myself to breathe as I tighten the laces,

I'm so agitated by what's about to come.

It's stupid to feel like this, I chastise myself. It's been twelve years, and anyway, it's never permissible to be afraid of the dark.

But the minute the lights go down, my mouth goes dry. I can make myself move through the cinderblock rooms, shining my flashlight onto faceless paper targets. I can make myself shoot perfectly, hearing only the dull *pop pops* through my earmuffs, but it doesn't matter. I still see that house, the terrified and blank face of the perp, spattered with Frazer's blood. I still smell old food and vomit and the coppery scent of my fiancé's life soaking into the old, stained carpet. I still remember Frazer's vacant stare.

I relive it every single time I'm forced to do this.

When I finish, I'm as empty as the magazine in my gun.

"Two hundred forty-six out of two fifty." The firearms sergeant grins at me as I'm taking off my vest. "That's a new personal best."

"Sure."

He laughs. "Don't act too excited now."

I try to give him a smile in return, but it feels all wrong on my face. Everything feels wrong.

Nothing will ever feel right again.

Making excuses, I stride quickly out of the training center and get to my unmarked car. I go back to my station and finish up for the day, staying a couple of hours late because I forget to look at the clock and can't seem to feel the time passing. Jace has gone home—the keys to his patrol car are hung back up, and I recognize every personal car left in the lot, meaning none of them are his.

Not seeing Jace makes everything worse—makes everything so bad that I just want to curl up and cry and cry and cry.

But I don't cry. I never do.

Somehow I make it out to my own car, with my portfolio and purse in the passenger seat and my phone in my hand. I've dialed Russo.

What the hell am I even doing? I don't know.

"Russo," Nicki answers in her familiar brusque way.

"Nicki, where do your evening people go to unwind?"

A pause. "Whyyyyyyy are you asking?"

"I'm looking for someone."

"Is it Jace Sutton?" my old friend asks in a too-casual voice.

Oh no. Like any cop, Nicki smells gossip, and I'm searching for a plausible reason—any plausible reason—why I'd need Jace after hours.

"I have a couple questions about his contacts today. He was out of the station his whole shift, and I didn't have a chance to catch him before he left." Even with as shaken up as I am, as empty and wrong-feeling, my voice is still perfectly steady, perfectly cool. I know I sound convincing.

"Okay," Russo says, and I can tell she's torn between her instincts and how well I sold that lie. "Well. The eves crew usually heads over to the Dirty Nickel after a shift or on their days off. He might be there, I guess."

Her guess is my hope. I don't have his cell number, and I don't feel comfortable digging through personnel records to get it when this isn't police business. Ditto with his address.

But showing up at his favorite dive is any better? Get a grip, Day.

"Thanks, Nicki."

"Anytime. And hey..." She stops for a moment, as if deciding how to proceed. "I saw in payroll that you had low-light range today. And I know that—well, what I mean is, if you ever need to talk, I'm here."

My throat feels as if someone's cinching a ribbon tight around it. "Thank you, Nicki. That's very kind."

"I mean it, okay?"

"Okay. Good night."

And Russo hangs up without saying goodbye, per usual. I drop the phone in my passenger seat and sigh.

I should go home.

I should go home and do what I've done every year after low-light range: pop open a bottle of wine, drink the entire thing, and then fall asleep curled around Frazer's college sweatshirt.

I should not go to a place called the Dirty Nickel to find a man thirteen years younger and...

And what? What is my plan? That Jace will take one look at me and know I need to be hugged? That I need a warm chest to finally, finally cry into?

No. If anything, we'll fuck, because that's the only connection we have, and then we'll both be miserable after because every time we have sex, we're courting major professional trouble.

I should not go to the Dirty Nickel.

I should not.

I start my car and tell myself to drive home.

♦♦♦♦

The Dirty Nickel is in a rougher part of town, in a cluster of old strip malls and used car lots, tucked away at the end of a low-slung building that also contains a thrift store and a vape shop. It's a far cry from the martini bar I occasionally venture out to with my girlfriends from college.

I nearly almost go home to change into something less fancy...and then remember I'm not in my usual silk and tailored wool. I'm in the dark-blue polyester of my uniform, with utility boots and a ponytail.

All I'm missing are the sunglasses and I could be a cop for Halloween.

With a sigh at the uniform—and at everything, absolutely everything—I get out of the car and walk inside. It doesn't matter what I'm wearing. It doesn't matter because I shouldn't be here, shouldn't be doing this, but it's the only thing I can think to do. It's the only thing that feels right when everything else feels so wrong.

The inside of the bar is only marginally better than the outside. Pool tables hunker down under dim lights, a couple of televisions play a baseball game between two teams no one cares about, and an unseen jukebox issues forth music the other detectives and I call "construction worker rock."

At seven, the place is just picking up, and I catch a table in the far corner with a few faces I vaguely recognize. Young cops. It's awful, perhaps even a little elitist, but I don't bother to learn a rookie's name until *they* bother to stick around for five years. Or more.

So I'm not entirely certain who they are or what shift they work or how long they've worked for Hocker Grove, but they're definitely HGPD. Even if I didn't recognize their faces, I'd be able to tell they were cops immediately. Legs sprawled but eyes alert, everyone in those free T-shirts you get for working golf tournaments or charity 5Ks or holiday parades. The men with short, inexpensive haircuts and the women in low ponytails or messy buns.

Not every woman.

In a table of about twelve, five are women, and three of those five are definitely cops, but the other two are just as definitely not. They've got impeccable makeup and glossy hair, and they're young, so fucking young.

Badge bunnies.

I've never liked the term—it seems vaguely sexist to me to disparage young women for the type of men they like to take to bed—but right now, something about their shiny, giggling youthfulness sets my teeth on edge. Especially after I see that one of them is curled around the one cop I *do* recognize.

Jace.

He hasn't seen me yet. He's peering up at the baseball game with his fingers wrapped around a beer bottle, but the bunny sees me standing in the doorway. She watches me watching them with her salon-perfect ombre hair brushing against Jace's shoulder and her hand on his thigh. He's in street clothes, the same kind of free-event T-shirt the rest of the cops are wearing, and battered jeans and boots.

And he still looks magnificent. All rounded, muscled shoulders, long, firm thighs, and a stubbled jaw that looks like pure sex. A warrior at rest, with the requisite maiden waiting to comfort him.

I have to go.

That's the only thought that registers in my mind—the rest is an awful kind of static. A static that hisses *what did you expect? You pushed him away. How long did you think it would take him to find someone else to screw?*

Oh God. I've made a giant mistake in coming here.

I'm turning to leave when he sees me, and it's like all the air is sucked from the room. His eyes meet mine, and I can't read them, can't even try, because there seems to be every feeling inside that silver gaze. Anger and hurt and lust and longing, and they're all directed at me. Right at me.

The bunny looks up to Jace as if she's trying to read his stare like I am, except she takes the extra liberty of sliding her hand up his thigh to rest against the unyielding contours of his abs. I think she also managed to graze his cock on the way up, and Jesus Christ, who was I kidding with that whole *if I break it off earlier, I won't be heartbroken* bit?

Because I did break it off early, yet here I am, feeling like someone's using the jaws of life to cut through my ribs and expose my beating heart. On top of what I went through today at range, it's too much.

It's too fucking much.

I break our gaze and wheel around, opening the door into the summer evening and making my escape.

I have to go.

I have to go home to my wine and to Frazer's sweatshirt and the loneliness I chose for myself. At least that way I can be vulnerable in front of nothing more important than a sweatshirt. At least I'm not making a scene in a begrimed bar in front of a whole table of cops.

And I can leave Jace to the bunny and the inevitable outcome of the night. She can kiss that pouty, serious mouth as bad music blares through the bar, and she can have those big hands drag her back to the bar bathroom for impromptu sex. She can feel the ruthless thickness of his cock wedging inside her. The hard flex of his abs and hips against her ass. His teeth biting her neck as he releases inside her.

They can have each other, and I'll have myself and an old sweatshirt that doesn't even smell like the man it used to belong to, and it will be fine.

The summer air is still hot, still waving above the pavement and trying to pull sweat out of my body. It feels like a punishment, and one I deserve.

The door opens again, and the cop in me can't help but turn at the knowledge someone's behind me.

"Cat." Jace's voice is husky. "What the hell are you doing here?"

"Going home," I say. I turn away from him because I can't look at him. I can't look at the man I pushed away, because I can't lie to myself and pretend I don't regret it. Pretend I feel some kind of wise, selfless pleasure in seeing some girl almost two decades younger than me crawl all over him.

A hand grabs my arm, and I'm spun to face him.

"The fuck you're going home," he says roughly.

I'm brittle, I'm so damn brittle, and I can't keep my tone even as I say, "I'm leaving and you're free to go back inside to your *friends*." My voice hitches over the word, and again that awful feeling of having my ribs cut open returns, even though I deserve it, even though I did it to myself.

"I don't want to go back inside to my friends," he says, clearly missing my implication in the word. "I want to know why you're here."

I twist myself out of Jace's grip and start walking to my car. "I shouldn't have come," I say, more to myself than him.

"But you did," he says as he follows me. "Why, Cat? Why did you come here?"

I have my car unlocked before I get to it so I can make a quick escape, but Jace isn't going to make it that easy for me. Before I can open the door, his hands land on either side of me, caging me in. The hot metal has to be uncomfortable, but there's no pain in his voice as he leans down to my ear.

"Tell me."

The moment seems to intensify, crystallize, and become something sharper, more vivid.

Cicadas are chirruping madly everywhere, and a breeze is blowing an empty soda can across the lot. It's so humid that the air is a heavy blanket over my skin, and behind me I can feel the press of Jace's body. His biceps crowding my shoulders. His chest against my back. His massive erection against my rear.

And then there's that scent. That leather and tea tree oil scent, and I hope it's rubbing on my clothes. I hope I smell like him when I get home.

That, more than anything, defeats me. How can I stay

strong when Frazer's sweatshirt smells like nothing and Jace is here and vibrant and alive and he smells like everything? How can I stay strong when I realize that maybe I want Jace more than I ever wanted Frazer...and how can I stay strong when I realize that *today*, of all days?

I hang my head forward in surrender.

"I came for you," I admit in a tired voice. "I came here to find you."

CHAPTER EIGHT

JACE

Hot, raw joy floods through my veins at her confession.

I open up the car door before she's even finished speaking. "Get in," I say shortly, and then I'm around the other side of the car in a heartbeat, climbing into her passenger seat after carefully setting her portfolio on the floor.

I'm already buckled by the time she manages to sit down. She doesn't start the car.

"Jace..."

"Ninety-three eleven Reeds Road," I say. "Unit ten. My place."

She bites her lip. "What about your friends inside?"

"My tab's paid," I reply. "And those assholes will be fine without me."

A little huff. "I'm not talking about assholes or your *tab*, Jace. I'm talking about the girl who was in your lap."

Oh. *Ohhhh.*

I look at her more carefully now, at the burnish of red along her cheekbones and the press of her lips. She's jealous. She's jealous, and that sends a whole stir of male pleasure swirling in my chest.

"I don't care about that girl because I'm leaving here with you. You're the one I'm taking home."

Her forehead makes contact with the steering wheel; for once, that perfect ballet posture is slumped. "This is a bad idea."

I touch her shoulder, the familiar fabric of the uniform made sweetly exotic over her slender, lithe muscles. And then I touch the pale silk of her thick ponytail because I can't resist it. "I'm not taking you back to my place to fuck you."

She lifts her head, eyes me warily. "You're not?"

"No." I'm still toying with her ponytail. I'm totally entranced by the sight of all that exquisite hair bundled into a rope that practically begs to be wrapped around my fist. "I'm taking you back to my place so I can take care of you. In a not-fucking way."

"I don't need taking care of," she says defensively, stiffening back up to her normal erect bearing. I can't play with her ponytail like this anymore, dammit, and I settle for curling a finger around her chin instead and making her look at me.

"You came here to find me and you found me, and now this is what's going to happen, okay? Start the car and drive, Cat. Drive us home."

I know she's wrestling with herself, nibbling more on that plush lower lip until she finally relents and starts the car. "Okay," she says. "But I don't have to stay."

"Of course not."

But of course she does.

I don't mean that in a nonconsensual way—she's free to leave whenever she wants—but in an emotional sense. I know she needs someone with her, and that someone should be me. I've seen this look in soldiers' eyes before. I've seen faces full of vacant restlessness. I don't know what happened to Cat today, but I know whatever did happen was Bad. Bad with a capital B.

And with a Bad thing, you can either shove that shit way down and hope nothing ruptures, or you can find someone you trust and find a way to bleed it out. Talking, drinking, fucking, music—anything is fair game.

I think Cat has been shoving her shit down for years, and I think she's finally rupturing. I want to be the one to help her bleed it out instead.

I don't even really know why—in no way should I feel like I deserve that place in her life or in her hurt and healing after just two screws—but I do. This week did nothing to slake my thirst for her. In fact, it just got worse and worse as the days rolled on without the chance to hold her slender wrists in my hand or the opportunity to run my thumb along the luscious lines of her mouth.

I jerked my dick raw thinking about her at night. I throbbed in mute agony as I sat across the meeting room table from her during the day. I wanted her so badly that I thought my bones might crack from it.

And don't get me started on what happens whenever I think of her words ending our little fling.

I look at you and I know that's not going to be possible for me.

I look at you and I think you might be capable of breaking my heart.

I think of those words—and let's be honest, I've probably thought of them every ten minutes since she said them—and this fierce, strange urgency comes over me, like I'm at the top of the roller coaster and ready for the plunge straight into danger. It makes my stomach twist up into my chest. And then something vital in my chest twists up into my throat. And then I just want to throw her over my shoulder and do something drastic. Abduct her like a Viking. Marry her. Hell, even cuddle her on the couch, which is something I haven't done in years and never thought I'd want to do again.

For now, though, I'm taking care of her. Whatever she needs is what I'll give, for as long as she'll let me.

"You're in uniform," I remark as Cat pulls out onto the street and angles the car toward my apartment. "I've never seen you in uniform."

"I had range today," she says, not taking her eyes from the road. "I'll wear the utility uniform for training and, you know, the dress uniform for the official department stuff." Her mouth gives a self-conscious twist. "I wear it so rarely that it almost feels like a costume now."

"When I first saw you standing there, I thought I was going to come in my pants."

My words are so surprising that she snorts out a very unladylike laugh, which makes me smile. I like seeing these cracks in her control, these glimpses of the warm, funny woman underneath her shell.

But I'm also not kidding. Cat in her silk shirts and high heels is a wet dream come to life, but Cat in uniform? I don't even have the words. It's like all that strength and resolve she normally hides under a veneer of cold dignity is even more on display, stripped down to the essential power and discipline she exudes.

The fitted lines of the shirt highlight her delicately squared shoulders and reveal the tight swells of muscle in her arms. The pants cling to her taut ass and legs. And her hair in that ponytail—without the gentle, Hollywood-starlet curtain of it softening her features, you can see exactly how ethereal she is. High cheekbones and big, fragile eyes. A comely jawline that ends in a pointed, adorable chin. Coupled with that booted, confident stance of hers and her svelte form, she could be one of those elves from the fantasy novels. Otherworldly and lethal. Deceptive beauty concealing deadly dominance.

God, what man doesn't want to tangle with that?

It only takes a few minutes to get to my house, which is one of the reasons I like the Dirty Nickel. It's a short ride home or only a medium walk, and while I'm not hung up on things being convenient in my life, I do like simple. Straightforward.

So what are you doing right now, then?

We park and get out, and then I lead her up the stairs to my door. It's only as I'm letting her in that I have a burst of sudden self-consciousness about how she will see my place. She of the flawlessly decorated bungalow. She of the kitchen piled with fresh fruit and flowers. She of the real-ass art hanging above her sofa.

What is she going to think when she sees my Craigslist couch and inherited recliner? My collection of signed baseballs and the empty QuikTrip cup on my counter I forgot to throw away this morning? I keep the place pretty tidy, but for all that, it's undecorated and shabby, and it looks like it belongs to a twenty-four-year-old guy without a girlfriend.

My cheeks flame as we walk inside, and I'm waiting for her to say something, waiting for her to raise a sculpted eyebrow at the place, but instead she just turns to me and goes straight into my arms. Without asking, without hesitation, as if she belongs there. And whatever has been twisting from my chest into my throat now twists so hard that the back of my eyelids are burning.

"Are you ready to talk about it? About what made you come find me?" I whisper into her hair.

Her face is buried in my chest, and she just shakes her head, a *swish swish* of that tempting ponytail.

"Can I take care of you, then? Without talking?"

A bob of the ponytail. *Yes.*

I wrap my arms around her slim frame, just taking a moment to relish the feeling of her crushed to me, so elegant yet so strong. And then I walk her backward in slow, careful steps to my bathroom, where I flick on the light and pick her up to set her on the counter.

She watches me with wide, red-rimmed eyes. She hasn't cried yet, but I can feel the force of her tears pushing against her restraint, flooding her control.

"Do you trust me?" I ask.

"Yes," she murmurs.

"I'll stop when you say. Always."

She blinks up at me, suddenly looking very young and very, very lost. "I know."

I take in a deep, shivering breath as I reach for her.

The thing is that our first time, and our second, Cat initiated. Cat told me her address or purred that she wanted to get fucked again, and then I followed where she led. I knew exactly what she wanted out of me, which was a big cock and a dirty mouth.

But now? Now when she's sought me out, looking like the sun's been darkened to ash? It's different. This isn't just a quick, hungry screw. This isn't a primitive urge let out to play. This is me giving something to her, not us trying to take from each other in a frenzied embrace, and I want to get it right. I want to get it so right that she trusts me to give it to her again and again.

I want her to always find me when she needs something. I want to always fix anything that's hurting her.

And now my throat is so tight I can barely breathe.

I begin unbuttoning her uniform shirt, taking care to keep my fingers from grazing against the silky fabric of her expensive athletic shirt underneath. Once I get the top few buttons undone, I can access the hidden zipper behind the placket of dummy buttons and unfasten the shirt all the way. I pull it from her arms and then drape it over the towel bar.

Next come her boots, which I unlace and gently remove, as if I'm handling glass slippers and not steel-toed footwear. She flinches when I get to her socks—I imagine in Cat's head, someone seeing and interacting with something as shamefully human as her socks is very embarrassing—but I don't let her move away. I'm not afraid of her socks. And nothing about her wonderful body should make her shy. After pulling the socks free, I give her bare feet several kisses to prove it.

I nudge her off the counter and remove her belt and pants, which also go over the towel bar, and now she's only in her undershirt and panties.

"Do you trust me?" I ask again, and she knows what I'm asking. Does she trust me not to make this sexual? Does she trust that I'm not doing this for me but for her?

She nods.

And then I strip her completely bare.

It's the first time I've seen her naked, and even though I ignore my erection, my body's response to her unclothed form is like being struck by lightning. Heat everywhere. Light behind my eyelids. My life poised on a razor's edge.

She's porcelain, rare and precious.

Her breasts are little teardrops, still pert and high on her chest and tipped with pale-pink nipples. A narrow waist curves in and then gently flares into her hips, and an adorable navel studs her belly along with a couple tempting freckles. Below that belly is the sweet cup of her pussy, covered by neatly—almost primly—trimmed blond curls.

But she's also so *real*. There's a few thin white streaks along her hips and on the sides of her breasts—the kind of stretch marks that come from living, not from babies—and a small curve below her navel that softens her belly out of true flatness. Slightly too-large areolas and a little mole under one breast.

She's real. And perfect.

I pull her into me and kiss her hairline because I can't not kiss it.

"You're so fucking beautiful it hurts to look at you," I say roughly.

She only rubs her face against my still-clothed chest in answer.

I step back and quickly undress, doing my best to ignore the throbbing erection currently aimed at the ceiling. I turn on the shower and coax her inside once it's warm.

I start washing her. Methodically, scrupulously. Avoiding the stiff buds of her nipples and the plump weight of her ass and the silky curls between her legs. Instead, I focus on her arms and her legs and her feet. I spend a long time soaping up her back and shoulders and then kneading her tight muscles until she's limp and heavy-eyed. The familiar smell of my body wash rises all around the shower stall, mixed with something fragrant and female that is uniquely her. I wish we had her soap here, her scents, but at the same time, I can't deny the primitive pleasure in having her covered in my own. Marking her skin with my smell.

After her body, I wash her hair.

I mean for it to be comforting, soothing, and maybe it is at first. As I pull her hair free from her ponytail with solicitous care—making sure not to yank or tug—and as I begin working the shampoo into her hair, she makes low, happy noises in her throat and leans back against me. For a while, it seems like she's practically purring under my touch, and I make sure to massage her scalp as I work. To pamper her.

But after I rinse the conditioner from her hair, I notice that her shoulders are hitching in barely perceptible jerks, rising and falling in the suppressed, shuddering way of someone trying to hide their tears.

She's finally letting it out.

"Cat, baby," I say, turning her so that she can bury her face in my chest again, which is what she does. I wrap my arms around her and cradle her, my broad back shielding us from the spray as she sobs against me and I stroke her hair. She cries so hard that her entire body shakes, that she can barely breathe, and I wonder if she cries like this often.

I wonder if this is the first time she's ever let herself cry about anything.

I chafe her back and kiss her wet hair that smells like my shampoo, and I simply hold her and let her use me. Use me as a safe place for her, use my arms and my chest and my silence. My strength and my body are hers. And I'm beginning to think my heart is too.

After a good ten or fifteen minutes, her sobs begin to space apart, quiet down into muted sniffles and sucks of breath, and she tilts her head to look up at me with owlish eyes still glassed over with tears.

"Thank you," she whispers. I can barely hear it over the running water.

I give her temple a kiss in response, using every last shred of my control not to kiss her full on the mouth and stroke her tongue with my own. In fact, we've both been very maturely ignoring my hard-on as it dug into her back and stomach, knowing it was a lost cause. I'm a little proud of how well-behaved I've been, considering the naked, slick, emotional circumstances.

"You said you weren't going to fuck me," Cat says, reaching

up to touch my face. I cradle her face in response, feeling the fragile flex and work of her jaw as she speaks. "What if I've changed my mind? And I want to be fucked?"

I peer down at her, water droplets dancing off my shoulders to make a heavy mist around us, and I study her expression through the haze. Study her aqua eyes, as open and vibrant as any tropical sea. Her mouth, which is currently in a shape of worried hope. Vulnerable excitement.

"We don't have to," I tell her. "I know I'm hard—that's just what happens when I'm around you—but that doesn't mean we have to do anything."

The elegant and refined Catherine Day gives me an eye roll worthy of any teenager. "Do I seem like the kind of woman who would give out pity sex just because a man had a sad, lonely boner?"

Hearing the word *boner* from her pretty lips is enough to make me laugh. "Okay, maybe not."

"I want to because I want to, Jace. Because I want you." Her eyebrows pull together a little, as if she's trying to puzzle something out. "I *need* you."

"Then you can have me," I rumble, sliding my palms down to the delicate bevel of her collarbone. And then down farther so I can feel her heartbeat under my fingertips and her nipples harden against my palms.

"Bare again," she begs as I start toying with them.

"Yes, ma'am," I murmur, and then I duck down and take her nipple into my mouth.

She gasps and arches, her hand coming to the back of my head to encourage me. I groan at the feeling of her fingers in my hair, tugging at the short locks, and I nearly growl at the sensation of her nipple stiffening even more between my lips.

I suck and suck with hot pulls, and then I catch it gently with my teeth until she gasps again. I move to the other side to torment her other one until they're both dark pink and jutting out from her breasts in inflamed need.

Then I drop to my knees.

Cat moans in anticipation as I brush my lips over her mound, and then she breathes out a long *ohhhhh* when my flickering tongue finds her clit. The shower has washed away most of her flavor, so I sling her leg over my shoulder and spread her open with my thumbs so I can taste the very heart of her.

I taste it, finally, with her pushed open and my face practically buried between her legs. I grunt as the sweet and salt of her blooms on my tongue, and my cock jolts with so much need that I have to jack it even as I service her just to keep my limbs from shaking.

"Oh God," she says once she catches sight of me handling my dick. "Oh God, get up here, get up here—"

I stand, careful to make sure she has her balance as I do, and then I press her against the shower wall and kiss the hell out of her. I kiss her until she can taste herself on my tongue, and I kiss her until she's trying to grind her pussy against the thigh I put between her legs.

I break the kiss and look down, thinking I could watch her needy pussy rocking against my bare thigh all day long, but of course my dick doesn't think that.

"Ready?" I ask.

She whimpers out a *yes*, and then I lift her into my arms so that her legs go around my waist, notch the head of my cock at her opening, and impale her in one smooth and delicious glide.

She wraps her arms around my neck for more leverage, and I brace her against the shower wall again. It's so much like the time we fucked in the station, except it's completely different. For one thing, it's slippery and wet, so we have to be more creative, fucking more with arms and twists of hips rather than with the grunting, battering force I used in the meeting room.

And instead of wearing the uniforms and badges that define our lives, we're stripped bare, right down to the skin. Even our expressions are naked, and Cat's is showing me all the fear and hurt and longing she carries around inside her every day, and her eyes are shining down at me like I single-handedly saved Christmas. There's a new kind of intimacy between us. Something more than sex—more than friendship or respect, even—and it feels fragile and breakable and beautiful beyond all reason.

Oh God. She's twisting me up so badly, twisting my heart right up.

I catch her lips with mine. "Do you..." I start to ask and then stop because what I was about to say was *Do you feel what you're doing to me?* And then maybe I would have also said, *Do you know I'm falling in love with you?*

I'm terrified of scaring her off, so I don't finish what I started.

And maybe I don't need to. Maybe Cat can see it in my face anyway, because she presses her forehead to mine and murmurs, "Yes."

Just that one word to my half question.

Do you...?

Yes.

I'm not going to survive her, I think.

She comes apart into a slippery, shivering mess, her cunt pulsating all around my shaft and squeezing me on to my own orgasm—as fierce as it is tender, surging into her warmth with her blue eyes on mine and her hand in my hair.

For a minute, we simply pant together like that, the water still spattering our shoulders and feet and our shared essences beginning to seep out from where we're joined. It's a surprisingly cozy feeling—or maybe cozy isn't the right word.

Restful, maybe. Familiar in the sense that it feels *right.*

In that I want to feel it again and again and again.

I comb her hair once we leave the shower and then bundle her into a big T-shirt of mine, and we nestle into my bed together. I'm too sated and sleepy and filled with this big new feeling for her to care that my bed is a store-closing-sale mattress on a plain metal frame or that my comforter is an old threadbare thing from my sister's college days. And Cat doesn't seem to notice. She just tucks her hands under her cheek like a fairy-tale princess and closes her eyes.

Not good enough.

I wrap an arm around her waist and pull her snug against my chest, allowing her to wriggle a bit so that her backside is pressed against my ever-present erection and her back is to my chest. I tell my dick to settle down, tuck her head under my chin, and completely encase her in my arms.

For a long time, we lie like this in the darkness, breathing together, her feet idly rubbing around my calves, and I think she's asleep. Until she takes a deep breath and says, "Frazer died at night. In a dingy little house in the bad part of town. The electricity had been shut off at some point, so when I went in, there were no lights on..."

She pauses, tensing in my arms, and I wonder what she's remembering. What she's seeing in her mind as she shares her pain with me.

"It was dark and so hard to see, and everything happened so fast. And Frazer—" She stops abruptly, and I guess that's a part of the story I won't get. At least not yet.

Another breath. "I shot, but I wasn't fast enough. It was dark, and I didn't want to hit the man I was going to marry."

I squeeze her close, knowing there's nothing I can say that will fix it.

"It was so stupid of me, but after...everything...I went outside to wait for backup, and there was blood everywhere, just everywhere. And it was starting to dry on my hands in this awful, sticky way, and all I wanted was to wash them, just *fucking wash them*, because all that blood was supposed to be inside *him*, not on *me*, and he was dead and I'd watched him die and it was all over my hands..."

"Cat. Babe." I hold her tighter, wishing there was some way I could cage her in my arms and keep her safe and free from bad memories forever.

"I did all the mandatory counseling after it happened, all the therapy for PTSD, and I'm fine most of the time. Nearly all of the time, in fact. But there's something about squeezing the trigger in the dark that makes it all come back."

I let her words fall back down around us like rain and soak into the ground. Soak back into silence. Sometimes that's all that's needed.

But this is something she and I share. Maybe we don't share an age or the same kind of upbringing, but tragic violence in the course of duty...yes. I know it too.

My voice is tired with experience when I speak. "Knowing you killed someone is hard. Knowing you didn't kill them fast enough to save someone you care about is even harder."

She considers this. "Did you kill anyone in the war?"

"Yes."

"And watched someone you care about die?"

"Yes. Not a fiancé, but a friend. Yes."

"Oh, Jace."

I press my lips into her hair. "It's okay. I did all the counseling too. And it's still hard, but I'm going to be okay."

Cat sighs. Rubs her toes on my shins. "I'm going to be okay too." And then more silence.

This time I think she's really drifted off, and I'm about to follow her, when she whispers, "Jace?"

"Hmm."

"Were you going to fuck that girl if I hadn't shown up?"

I don't know what it says about me that I'm a little glad she's still jealous, even though I left that girl in the cold so I could bring Cat home instead. Even though it was Cat who got her hair washed and then had my tongue in her pussy.

But I want her to know the truth. I want her to know where this is going for me. "No, I wasn't going to fuck her, no matter what happened. She's a friend's sister, so I didn't want to shove her off of me in public and embarrass her, but I planned on letting her know it wasn't going to happen."

"Why not?" Cat asks, and she asks it almost like she's afraid to hear the answer.

"I think you know why not," I reply. There's a long pause, and I may not have a ton of experience with delicate talk like this, but I know I've gone as far as I can go tonight. "Good night, Cat," I add softly, and she nestles her nose into my bicep in response.

And this time we really do fall asleep.

CHAPTER NINE

CAT

I wake up still wrapped in Jace's arms, with an almighty erection wedged against my bottom and soft snores in my ear.

The sun is bright and new, telling me it's still fairly early, and the lack of any alarms chiming in the room reminds me that we both have the day off. I stretch my legs and arms and back as much as possible inside his giant bear hug, wonder if I could possibly doze back off, and then reluctantly concede that I'm awake for good now.

I pry myself free of his embrace and make to slide out of bed and investigate Jace's coffee or tea options—but I'm immediately seized and hauled back against his big, sleepy body.

"No," comes his half-awake growl. "Stay."

"It's morning, Jace."

"It's our day off." His voice is petulant, adolescent even, and I roll over to look at him, to coax him awake, but I'm simply crushed back into his chest. I can feel the snores vibrate through him when he falls back asleep seconds later.

"*Young* man," I whisper to myself, smiling a little. I manage to push away enough that I can stare at him—really stare at him—as he sleeps. At the adorable sprawl of his big body, the pout of his parted mouth, and the long eyelashes resting dreamily on his cheeks. All those handsome features, normally so severe, normally so stormy and scowly, are relaxed into a boyishly sweet expression in his sleep. He barely looks twenty-four like this, and you'd never guess he's a cop or a former soldier. You'd never guess he's known grief or fear or anger. That he's haunted by the memories of war.

He looks gentle and dear and young. So young.

I try to get out of bed again, this time more because I need a moment to process my feelings. About this young man, about how tenderly and thoroughly he made love to me last night. About how he wanted to take care of me beyond sex and outside it, before he even knew what was wrong.

Do you...?

Yes.

Even now, I'm not sure exactly what he was going to say, but it didn't matter. Whatever he wanted to know, the answer was yes.

This is skidding off the rails fast, Cat.

But I never do get a chance to process my feelings. I'm grabbed again, and this time Jace wakes up enough to put that massive erection to good use.

♦♦♦♦

For two weeks, I am unbearably, abominably weak, and for two weeks, Jace and I fuck constantly.

And everywhere. We fuck everywhere.

At my place. At his place. Twice more in the station—after

the brass went home this time. In his car, in my car, in the bathroom of an office building after interviewing a witness.

And every night as I fall asleep with his arms around me and his lips pressed to my neck, I think *you have to stop this—you have to end this pointless fling because it's going to hurt one or both of you.* It's unprofessional to have sex with a coworker, and it's a fireable offense to do it on duty, *and* it's just...unseemly, given his age.

Catherine Day doesn't do unseemly things! It isn't me, this torrid, sex-fueled affair, yet every time I convince myself to end it, something else happens and my resolve vanishes like it never existed in the first place. Jace will yank me into a searing, movie-worthy kiss or send me a heated gaze from the passenger seat of my car. Or he'll rumble *Cat, baby* in that husky growl of his, and nothing else will matter. Not our jobs or my reputation or seemliness. The only thing that matters is him and how close I can get my body to his in the next thirty seconds.

But despite the sex and the snuggling in bed and the occasional domestic moment of making coffee or dinner together, there's not another vulnerable moment like there was that night in the shower. I don't cry, he doesn't ask *do you...?,* and we don't talk about our pasts again. We have sex and talk about the case. Professional and age considerations aside, it should be perfect.

Why isn't it perfect?

Why do I keep thinking about that moment in the shower? Why do I keep wishing he'd finished his question?

Keep hoping he'll ask it again?

My confusion isn't helped any by Kenneth, who's been trying to corner me into dinner for a few weeks now. Would I say yes if I weren't screwing Jace? *Should* I still say yes? I mean, Jace and I haven't defined what we are to each other, and it's not like he's the loquacious type and full of effusive raptures about how much he adores me. For all I know, that night in the shower was a fluke and I really am just a convenient lay. For all I know, I'm just a fun way to pass the time until something better comes along.

But.

But.

Even though the entire thing is ridiculous, even though I'm worse than foolish for carrying on with a man so much younger than me, I can't bear to entertain even the thought of another person while I'm with Jace. Maybe I'm being too romantic or overly monogamous, or maybe it's some kind of transferred loyalty from Frazer, who was the last cop I dated before Jace—but whatever the reason, I won't start something with Kenneth. I don't even want to.

I call him back and agree to dinner, deciding I owe him this conversation face-to-face. I won't tell him about Jace—certainly not—but I'll tell him there's someone else right now. It will be a hard conversation to have, but Kenneth will understand. I doubt he spent his three years in St. Louis pining for me, and surely he didn't expect to come back and find me pining for him.

But now it's nearly time for that dinner—just a few hours away—and I still haven't told Jace that I'm going out with Kenneth.

He won't understand, I think.

But you know that he'd want to know about it anyway, I argue with myself, and then I sigh. I'm thirty-seven, and I'm obsessing over boy drama like I'm in junior high. What the hell has gotten into me?

With a sigh and a quick press of my fingertips against my forehead to help alleviate some of the pressure building there, I refocus on the files in front of me. I've been combing through them ever since our last two leads ran dry.

In a case as big as this, there's always another lead. Always another angle. I just have to find it.

I'm deep into the file on the last burglary—the one where I met Jace—and I'm clicking through the photos on my laptop when I hear a deep voice ask, "Drywall?"

Startled but happy, I turn to see Jace leaning against the edge of my cubicle, looking like a cop from a cop calendar with his crossed arms showing off biceps and forearms and his pretty mouth lifted into the tiny crook that passes for a smile for him.

"Drywall?" I ask back, trying to think through the temporary haze of electric lust and happiness that descends upon me every time I see him.

He tilts his head at my desk. "You were staring at your laptop, muttering 'drywall, drywall' at the screen."

"Oh." I turn back to my desk to make a quick note while gesturing for him to come in. "I hadn't realized I was talking out loud. How was the warehouse search?"

"Nothing there," Jace says and takes a seat in the spare chair next to me. He brings the chair close enough that our knees touch under my desk, and I want to melt. I want to run my fingers along the cut hardness of his thigh up to the heavy cock currently pushing at his zipper.

I don't. But the temptation is agonizing.

"Any chance they could have moved the televisions before you got there?" I ask, forcing myself to focus on the task at hand. I sent Jace to check out a couple locations that had been used to hide stuff like this before. A shot in the dark but worth looking into.

Jace shakes his head. "One warehouse is being renovated into lofts, and the place was crawling with a construction crew. No one I talked to had seen anything being moved in or out. The other was completely abandoned but had a few squatters staying inside. They swore up and down they hadn't seen any trouble."

"They would say that," I murmur, but I trust Jace's instincts—for now.

"And the drywall?" Jace asks.

I frown back at the screen. "I'm not sure yet. There's just something about all that drywall dust at the scene that keeps tugging at me. It will come."

"Mm," Jace says, and from the way he says it, I can guess the word *come* sent his mind in a very different direction than police work.

I'd roll my eyes, but that wouldn't be very fair of me since I've spent the last five minutes vaguely considering pulling him back into the meeting room for a quick round to help me last the rest of the day. The day that I'm—sigh—spending part of with Kenneth.

Tell Jace. Tell him now. He'll be pissed, but he'll be less pissed than if he finds out later.

I open my mouth to speak, but Jace gets there first. "I have my niece's birthday party this evening," he says quickly, almost as if he's blurting it out. "It's nothing super formal, just a barbecue and cake at my sister's house, but I thought you could come with me. And, um. You know." He looks down at his boots, suddenly bashful and boyish and so...un-Jace-like.

The first time I ever drove a car faster than one hundred miles per hour, I was in academy and terrified beyond all reason. Yet there was this moment as I accelerated—adrenaline screaming through my veins, and my stomach back where I left it at the starting line—when my heart floated in my chest out of sheer, exhilarated joy.

I feel that now.

Jace's invitation to meet his family and the unusually shy way he asked—it makes me feel like I'm driving one hundred miles per hour, with my heart hammering fast and happy even as my body registers unheard of terror.

Because I know what happens when you drive fast.

You brake hard.

I can't meet his family tonight because I have to have dinner with Kenneth, and anyway, it would be ludicrous for me to meet his family. How would I even introduce myself? As the coworker he's been jeopardizing his job with because we can't seem to wrangle our hormones under control? As the cougar who caught his poor, innocent body in her claws?

Jesus.

No. I can't meet his family and his parents, who will only

awkwardly be a decade or so older than myself.

And I shouldn't meet them because we aren't a *thing* anyway. We aren't going to be together for long, because these flings never last, and then when his family doesn't see me again, they'll know for sure that I was the predatory sex-harpy taking advantage of their handsome son.

All the euphoria, the heart-floating-in-my-chest, it just stops, like I really have mashed on the brakes with all my weight. And I suddenly very much want to cry.

I glance at his face, with its red of embarrassed hope burnishing his cheeks, and hate myself. "Jace, I'd love to go, but—"

"It's okay," he says, very fast. "It's okay. I didn't really think you'd want to go anyway, and I only thought it would be an easy way to get dinner and stuff, so—"

He's killing me. My cubicle has become the scene of a homicide.

"Stop," I say, grabbing his hand and hating myself even more for the white lie I'm about to tell. "It's just that I've made plans with a friend for dinner already. But I will see you tonight at my place after? Just let yourself in through the garage if you get there before me."

"Sure," he says, and there's so much in his voice, so much that isn't normally there for this quiet, primal cop, and I think my heart is breaking. And that's almost the scariest part of this.

I've gotten to the point where his unhappiness is more painful than my own.

♦♦♦♦

Kenneth and I meet at one of the understatedly elegant restaurants that suits us both so well, and it's as I'm walking in that my work phone rings.

"Day," I answer after I fish it out of my purse.

"Hey," comes the person on the other end. "This is Jessica in Dispatch. We just had a woman call in trying to speak to you. She says she works at one of the doctors' offices that's been robbed and needed to check something on the missing items report."

I see Kenneth at a far table, already with a bottle of wine on the table, and I give him a small wave before I turn away. "Did she leave a number?"

"She did. I'll email it, along with the call notes. She sounded pretty upset about something, but she only wanted to talk to you."

That isn't unusual. Speaking to the detective on a case is like speaking to the manager at a store—there's an imagined aura of authority cloaking the interaction. And I certainly wouldn't turn down the opportunity to talk to anyone directly. Our dispatchers are good, but there's a limit to what they'll be able to lift out of a conversation if they're not familiar with a case. And at this point, I need every lead I can get.

After confirming that she'll email the details, I hang up with Jessica and then make my way over to Kenneth, who stands to greet me.

"Cat," he says warmly, taking my elbows and kissing me on the cheek. It's shocking how unpleasant it feels, how very wrong to be kissed by someone who's not Jace, and I'm quiet as I take my seat, trying to process the tumult of troubled feelings currently jostling around in my chest.

You're a detective, Cat. You know how to read evidence.

Being irritated at Kenneth's touch combined with how miserable I felt today turning down Jace's invitation seems to point toward a very obvious conclusion. One I don't want to think about because what it means is too maudlin. Too destabilizing.

Far too real.

"I'm so glad you could meet me," Kenneth says as he pours me a glass of sauvignon blanc.

I take it gratefully, determined to fortify myself before the hard conversation starts. "Thank you for being patient while we were making plans. This case has been eating up lots of my evenings." *Well, the case and sex marathons with a man almost half your age.*

Kenneth waves the hand holding his own wineglass, in a *don't even worry about it, I totally understand* gesture, and I can't help but fixate on that hand. On the difference between his manicured fingers under the pale wine and how Jace's fingers looked wrapped around a beer bottle at that bar a few weeks ago. How casually masculine Jace was. How unselfconscious.

Kenneth pretends to be casual too, with his air of careless sophistication, but his mannerisms are too studied for that. The wine label faced outward so the rest of the diners can see that he spent eighty dollars on a single bottle. The angle of his shoulders so that his thin sweater over his button-down will pull just the right way over his arms and back to display his physique.

I think of that date three years ago and the terrible sex

that followed—the kind of sex you'd expect from someone who focuses more on style than substance.

This is the person I thought made the most sense for me?

We make small talk for a while, mostly about work and his daughters, and then we hem and haw over whether we want to order the rabbit or the octopus, because that's the kind of restaurant this is. I wait until after we eat and after Kenneth has his third glass of wine to turn the conversation to our non-future.

"Kenneth," I start, searching for tact. "You're a good friend, and—"

"Oh, Cat," he says and reaches for my hand across the table. "I thought you'd never broach the subject. I don't want to dance around this because I think we are both too old and too tired for that, don't you?"

I hate the way my hand feels in his. How funny that Jace can bend me over a table and plug my ass with his thumb while I babble incoherent, orgasmic *thank yous*...and yet the peremptory way Kenneth takes my hand in a public building raises my hackles.

I gently remove it, giving him a small smile. "I agree."

"I like you," he continues, although he stares at his own hand with a furrowed brow, as if confused about what just happened. "I know our last foray into romance was interrupted by my move to St. Louis, but I'm here to stay now, Cat. And I want to make a new life here. Find a partner to share that with. Do you understand what I'm saying?"

I do understand. He's thinking exactly what I've thought before: the two of us make sense on paper. We're the logical and inevitable pairing of upbringing and profession. Two rich kids who caught a case of conscience and went into the field of justice instead of finance or medicine or literally anything else more lucrative? That's us. We'd be able to kvetch about judges and defense attorneys while we shopped for antiques and took winery tours.

But in the last few weeks, I've discovered I don't want that...if I ever did.

"I understand, Kenneth, and three years ago I might have wanted to be that partner," I say. "But that's not why I came here tonight."

A hard anger passes over his features so quickly that someone less perceptive might have missed it. But I catch it.

I catch it, and I'm suddenly beyond grateful that I'm not going to entwine my life with his. Not when his first response to rejection is anger. Not when all my cop senses are currently on high alert at the prospect of a man so much larger than me suffering from the side effects of a fragile ego.

Fortunately, that ego appears to value public perception over personal slights, because he doesn't seem inclined to make a scene. Instead, he takes a deep pull from his wineglass and leans back in his seat. "Is there someone else?"

"There is."

He looks off into the middle distance and then looks back to me after a long, pensive moment. "Why did you come to dinner tonight, Cat?"

"I came because I respect you and I thought this conversation deserved care and attention."

He sighs, rubbing his forehead, and then gives me a

rueful kind of smile. "That's how you know we're old, by the way. Seven years younger and you would've just DMed me on Twitter. Seven years younger than that, and it would've been a passive-aggressive Snapchat story."

I laugh a little and so does he, and my tension slowly ratchets down.

He's taking it okay. It's going to be okay.

"I am sorry," I say. "I truly enjoyed the time we spent together before you moved. But then I met"—I stumble, almost saying Jace's name and only barely catching myself in time—"someone, and I'd like to see where things go."

Kenneth shakes his head, seeming sad. "I should've reached out earlier. It's my loss, Cat. I hope he makes you happy."

I don't miss the bitter edge in his tone, and my cop senses prickle again. Outwardly, he seems like he's adjusting well, but there's something emanating from him that makes me uneasy. I never ignore these instincts, and I feel abruptly grateful that I drove here on my own and don't have to rely on him for a ride home.

"Thank you," I say. "He does make me happy."

There must have been too much truth in my tone, because there's more irritation in Kenneth's expression now. Luckily the waiter comes by with the check. Kenneth and I politely argue about who will take the bill—a pointless argument because the money isn't significant to either of us. We agree to split it, and then we pay and make to leave.

Kenneth catches my hand a last time after we stand up, and he kisses the back of it. "I hope we stay friends."

"Of course," I say, but I doubt it.

In fact, I'll probably make sure to put some distance between us...at least until his bitterness fades and I sense he's safe again.

I get in my car and text Jace.

I really need you tonight.

And I mean sex—always that—but I think I might also mean more. I need his chest to bury my face in and his hands petting my hair. I need to tell him everything about Kenneth and apologize for not telling him sooner.

I need him to know that I only want him.

And I think I need to know that he only wants me. I think I need to be spanked, mounted, and fucked. I think I need all Jace's intensity centered on marking my body as his. I think I need my choices anchored in this raw connection Jace and I can't seem to shake.

I'm pondering all this as I drive home, chewing over the dinner and my uncomfortably big feelings for Jace, and I'm so wrapped up in my own thoughts that I don't notice anything different when I park my car in the garage and walk inside my kitchen.

"Have a good time?" says a low voice from behind me.

CHAPTER TEN

JACE

I almost didn't believe it when I saw them through the window. The restaurant they were at is in this fancy mixed-use development thing—the same complex that houses the bakery that made my niece's cake. I volunteered to pick up her cake so my sister could focus on getting everything else ready, and then I saw Cat's car—with the license plate number I couldn't help but memorize the first time I saw it.

I thought I'd pop in and say hi because that's where I'm at right now. I'm at the point where two hours away from her is bone-cutting agony, and I needed a fix. I'd just pop in, fake a smile to whatever martini-drinking girlfriend she was with, and then lean in to kiss her cheek. I'd smell her hair and her skin as I whispered what I was going to do to her later tonight. Where I was going to fuck her. How hard she would come.

But there was no martini-swilling girlfriend.

Instead, she sat across the table from Kenneth—fucking *Kenneth*—who looked handsome as always in his "only the best from JoS. A. Bank" way. And they were talking. And smiling. And drinking wine.

And the *rightness* of them in there tore through me like a

shotgun blast. Because of course Cat looked like a movie star with her expensive clothes and soft blond hair and those high heels that give her feet that glamorous, Barbie-style arch. And of course she looked like she belonged there with a man who knew what kind of wine to order, what kinds of arts events and charities to make small talk about.

Fuck.

And she lied to me about it.

Double fuck.

I should have left immediately. I should have stepped away and shelved this for a later discussion, but I didn't. I stayed and watched for another ten minutes, jealousy and hurt pounding through my veins. I stayed until my sister called and asked me what was taking so long with the cake.

It wasn't a surprise that I wasn't much in the mood for a party after that. I went, gave little Abigail her cake and her present and a big hug, and then decided to go home.

Which was when I got her text.

I really need you tonight.

I leaned my head back against the driver's seat and tried to talk myself out of it. I could cancel. I could tell her I wasn't feeling well, or that my sister needed help with the babies, or even that I saw her out with another man and didn't feel much like fucking tonight.

Which would be a lie. I want to fuck her now more than ever.

I want to feel her body pressed against mine. Feel her mouth moving over my own. I need to reassure myself with thrusts and moans and searching fingers that I'm not imagining what's between us. That she is still mine.

No. No fucking. Not until you've figured this out.

So I'm at her house because she asked and because it needs to be figured out. Even though the thought of *figuring it out* sends fear bolting through me like jagged sparks of lightning.

What if we *figure it out* and that is the end of us?

I pace through her sleekly renovated bungalow until I can make sense of my feelings. Until I can admit to myself that *falling in love* somehow turned into *being in love* without me realizing it, and now I have to deal with it. I have to admit to myself that us ending would destroy me.

She has to know.

But I won't be a dick. I'm here because she asked me to be. I'll tell her I know about Kenneth, and then I'll tell her how I feel. The choice is hers. I've been here before, after all, with Brittany and her reverse harem of jackasses who worked in cell phone stores or did car detailing or whatever it was that kept them here and available and not off fighting a war. I survived that with a woman I thought I might marry. I could definitely survive this.

Even if it doesn't feel like it.

Even if it feels like I already love Cat an infinite amount more than I ever loved Brittany.

Face it. You're in way deep. Deeper than you've ever been.

When Cat walks through the door, I don't mean to scare her, but that's what happens. I speak, and she spins in a sharp turn, her hand dropping to her hip as if she's reaching for her duty weapon.

Shit. I'm a dirtbag. I take a step back, my hands in the air like a suspect.

"Christ, Jace," she says, her hand falling away from her hip and her posture going from alert to its usual straight-backed poise. "You frightened me."

"I'm sorry," I say, and I mean it. "I didn't mean to...loom."

She sets her purse down on the counter and presses her fingertips against her forehead for a minute. "No, I—I should have remembered you might get here before me. I was just distracted."

By Kenneth? I want to ask, but I'm not going to. If I'm brutally honest with myself, we've never talked about being exclusive. We've never set any parameters around our relationship. Yes, fine, I'm still jealous as fuck, but I know I don't really have the right to be.

But I've underestimated Cat and her powers of observation. She gives me a once-over with those sea-blue eyes, with one delicate eyebrow arched and her lips pursed, and then she says, "You know I was with Kenneth."

God help any suspect who tries to lie to her.

"Yes," I say. "I know."

She looks at me almost like...like I don't know. Like she's disappointed. But disappointed in what? That I know? That I admitted it? Am I not being as calm as I think I am?

I take another step back, trying to reassure her that I'm not going to give her a hard time. That I'm not going to try to use my body to intimidate her. Her gorgeous, pressed-together lips grow more disapproving.

Does she want me to talk more? I don't trust myself to talk

more. I don't trust myself not to blurt out *you're mine, you're fucking mine,* drop to my knees, shove up her skirt, and prove it with my mouth. Prove that her body already knows who it needs, and it's not Mr. Men's Wearhouse. It's me.

"I thought you'd be jealous," she murmurs, still studying me.

"I *am* fucking jealous," I say tightly and then snap my mouth closed so fast my teeth click. *Don't be a dick, don't be a dick, don't be a dick.*

She takes a step forward. Another and then another while I stay completely still, unsure of what she's thinking.

"Prove it," she says, folding her arms across her chest.

"Excuse me?"

"Prove you're jealous."

It's like I'm in some alternate dimension—one where my primal, Freudian id makes all the rules. "I'm not sure what you're asking."

She sighs, suddenly looking very much like an impatient schoolteacher, which is not helping the angry lust roiling in my belly in the least. "What do you want to do to me right now, Jace?"

"I don't—"

Another step forward. "You want to screw me in the heels I wore to dinner with him? You want to handcuff me to the bed so I can't leave until you say I can?" She presses a hand against my chest. "You want to see your come on my stomach? Or my tits?" Her hand drops down to my belt, and I catch her wrist before it can go somewhere farther down.

I can't tell if she's in earnest or she's goading me. "Stop it."

"Why are you asking me to stop?" she asks. "Is it because you actually don't want this? Or is it because you doubt I'm really asking you for it?"

"Of course I doubt it," I say through clenched teeth. "What I really want would terrify you."

She gives a beautiful, rich-girl scoff. "Try me."

I lift a hand and slide it though her silky hair, fisting it at the base of her neck and holding her head back just enough that she won't be able to move without disrupting her balance. And then I lean in so my lips brush the shell of her ear as I speak. "I do want to fuck you in these heels. And in handcuffs. I want to fuck your mouth, and then I want to bend you over my knee and redden your ass until you think of me every time you sit down. I want you to take me everywhere in your body—and I mean *everywhere,* Cat—until you feel as owned by me as I'm owned by you."

Confident my little speech has frightened some sense into her, I let go of her hair and pull back. But instead of seeing her face tight with fear, I meet eyes with pupils blown wide with lust and blushing cheeks and her tongue working at her lower lip in a kind of fervent anticipation.

"You feel like I own you?" she whispers, searching my face.

"Isn't it obvious?" I ask.

She just keeps blinking up at me, like she can't believe it. Like she can't believe I feel it, and I trace that doubtful mouth with my fingertip as I speak.

"And I may be young, but I know what I want, Cat. I want you. I want to make you mine."

Her hand goes back to my belt, toying with it, but her eyes stay glued to mine. "Then make me yours, Jace. Right now. I won't break, I'm not"—a small smile here, as if at some private joke—"I'm not a china doll."

I consider her, reading her body's signs. Her nipples poking through her blouse trying to get my attention. Her pulse thrumming at the base of her neck. The blush below her collarbone that disappears down into that sexy silk shirt. She likes it when I'm possessive. Jealous, even. I remember that from the first time we had sex at the station.

But this is something different. "You're asking me to claim you," I say, making sure we're on the same page. "While I'm angry and hurt and jealous. While I want to be rough."

"Yes," she moans, pressing her breasts against my chest as her hand wraps around my denim-clad erection.

And that's all I can take. All the permission I need. I scoop her up and sling her over my shoulder, just like the Viking I wanted to be a few weeks ago, and smack her ass hard as I walk toward her bedroom. I feel her stomach hitching where it presses against my shoulder, and for a moment I wonder if she's crying or trying to speak, but then I hear—

She's laughing.

She's happy.

It's a roller-coaster laugh, the kind of laugh that's pulled out of you by adrenaline and joy and terror all mixed together, and I take it as extra confirmation that she's on board. I still say over my shoulder, "Say stop when you need to stop, baby."

Her voice is full of smug cop pride when she answers, "Fine. But I won't need to."

I don't think she will either. She's tough, tougher than anyone gives her credit for, and I think under all that good breeding and money is a woman who wants to test her limits. Who wants the edgy, filthy, primitive challenges no one else has known to give her.

But I know. I know what she needs.

I drop her onto her bed without warning, without delicacy, without even flicking on a light, and then I fall on her like a predator in the dark. I nip at her jaw and throat until she whimpers, and then I eat her mouth with stark, brutal kisses until both of us are breathing hard and my dick is leaking all over the inside of my jeans.

Taking her wrists in one hand, I pin them above her head as I grind into her clothed pussy with merciless hips. "How much did this cost?" I say, working a hand between us to pluck at her silk blouse. "Two hundred? Three hundred?"

"Three hundred," she pants.

It'll be hell on my bank account to replace, but so fucking worth it. I let go of her wrists and move up so I'm straddling her hips, and then I take one side of the blouse in each hand. She's wearing it in her usual way, unbuttoned to expose just the right amount of décolletage, and the fashionable part of the placket gives me just the right handholds to grab and tear the blouse apart.

It's a well-made shirt, and it takes plenty of strength to rip the buttons from their moorings and send them scattering across the bed, but I manage, revealing a lacy bra and Cat's stomach, both ivory-pale in the moonlight streaming through her window.

She looks wrecked like this, wrecked already, with her shirt rumpled and torn around her breasts and her hair mussed and her lips swollen from my attentions. I run my fingers over the swells of her lace-covered tits and down to her quivering belly. "All this is mine," I tell her.

"Yes," she says.

I move off her. I find the zipper to her skirt and yank it down with impatience, peeling the fabric from her body and tossing it on her floor like I don't know it probably also cost an unthinkable amount of money. And before I straddle her again, I allow myself to appreciate the vision she makes like this, with her white garter belt highlighting the nip of her waist and her nude stockings giving off a faint sheen in the moonlight. With her heels still curving her feet into sexy, chic arches.

She looks expensive. Cultured.

And I'm the man who gets to bite and bind and dishevel it all. I'm the man who gets to make her mine.

I remove the remains of the blouse from her and then straddle her again to knot her crossed wrists in the fabric. There's plenty of it, and it's soft and thick enough that I can bind her tightly, and I do, relishing the jagged exhale she gives when she tests the knot and finds it unyielding.

"Now," I say, climbing off her. "Let's see what the queen keeps in her toy box, hmm?"

With as much sex as we've had in the last few weeks, we still haven't dipped into her toy collection, although I know it's in her end table, and I know she must have some things in there that are at least mildly shocking, because she blushes whenever I ask her about what she has.

Well, there's no time like the present to find out.

I leave her trussed up on the bed while I make my way to her nightstand and pull open the drawer. I growl when I see what's inside.

"Dirty girl," I say, holding up the cool metal of a jewel-ended butt plug for her to see. I toss it on the bed, along with the bottle of lube she has stashed inside the drawer. "So fucking dirty. I knew you were. Knew you were keeping all kinds of secret filth wrapped up in all that silk."

She makes a needy noise and drops her bound hands to her stomach, and I only realize why when I see her fingers sliding under her panties to get at her pussy. I'm back on the bed in an instant, pinning her arms above her head again.

"Bad," I tell her. "You're doing bad things when you should be trying to be very good for me right now."

"Just make me come first," she demands, trying to rock her hips against my erection. "Make me come, and then I'll be good."

"Nice try," I rasp, biting her breasts until she listens. "You are mine right now, which means your orgasms are mine too. And you're not going to come until I know you're very, very sorry."

"Sorry for what?" she asks breathlessly.

"For making me want you so much. Now *shhh*."

I go back to the drawer and riffle through all the interesting items in there. In addition to the jeweled plug, she has a vibrating one, along with a very realistic dildo—which I'm boorishly proud of being bigger than—and three different vibrators. I pick a vibrator and then join her on the mattress, where she's currently trying to rub her thighs together for friction.

I pinch her nipple. "Knock it off."

"Make me come."

I pinch again, giving it a tiny twist through the lace this time. She gasps and then moans.

"Jace, please," she begs. "Just once, and then you can do whatever you want."

I don't bother responding to her ridiculous demand. I'm already too wrapped up in how *I* want her to come. How I want to stake my claim all over her body until it's mine, mine, mine.

I take the vibrator, turn it on, and lie on my side next to her, propped up on one elbow so I can watch her reaction as I buzz it over her nipples and navel. As I run it along her inner thighs and ghost it over her folds until her pleas start falling out of her mouth faster than her breaths.

She'll do anything, she says, anything I want. She'll suck me, jerk me, take me anywhere in her body, she'll do any depraved thing I ask...as long as I let her come right now. So long as I ease her misery just a little.

"No," I say simply.

But I do find her clit with the vibrator and give her a little taste—just a little hope—before I click the vibrator off and deny her again.

She writhes on the bed, trying to free her wrists from the blouse I tied around them, which is when I flip her onto her belly and prop her up on her elbows and knees.

"I like the thought of you with these plugs in your drawer, dirty girl," I say. I unhook her garters and garter belt and fling them to the floor. Her panties are lace, real and delicate, and it takes nothing for me to rip them off. And finally, I get the view I've been wanting all day. A cunt so wet it glistens in the near darkness and the tight star of her asshole above it.

I press a thumb against that star now, testing its tight resistance. "I like the thought of you so desperate for it here that you do it to yourself. That you squirm in bed alone at night, just needing it. My filthy baby."

She's moaning now and trying to push back against my touch.

"Have you ever really been fucked here, Cat? With a cock?"

"N-No," she answers, still seeking out more pressure and friction from me. "Just toys. But I—I want it. Wanted it for so long."

"None of those rich boys knew what to do with you, did they? They didn't know how shameless you really are. How much you need to sin." I palm her cunt, feeling how wet my words have made her, and she shudders at the contact.

"Jace," she pleads.

"Baby, you know the only answer you're gonna get is *when I'm good and fucking ready*, so instead of asking, why don't you tell me how you feel? What's happening inside that amazing mind of yours?"

"I-I feel like my skin is too tight," she manages, still trying to buck against my hand. I use my other hand to toy with her clit a little to reward her for obeying. "My cunt feels hollow. My nipples hurt, they're so hard. I feel like I haven't come in a thousand years."

I frankly feel the same way, with her wrists tied and her pussy against my palm, and I have a dizzying moment when I realize that my anger and my jealousy have turned into something else, something different. Like desire—but darker, because it's the desire to see her fall apart for me like I'm falling apart for her. Like possession—but better because she's begging to be possessed.

If I had to call it anything, I'd say it was love. Rough and elemental, the only love I'm capable of giving.

Ah fuck. I can't spin this game out for much longer. Not when the urge to claim her and to love her is pounding through me so hard that my cock throbs in time with it.

I take the plug in my hand, admiring its weight and its cute little jewel at the end, before I trace the cool tip of it down the curve of her spine.

She shivers.

"Plug first," I say. "Then me. And when I'm inside your ass for the first time—that's when you can come."

She gasps when she feels the cool drizzle of lube on her and again when I add the extra coolness of the plug pressed against her rim.

"Okay?" I ask, meaning all of it. "Need to stop?"

"No, no," she says. "Just—I usually warm it up first."

I test it with my finger and find that the metal is already warming up against her skin, so I decide I can push her a little here. "I'll give you something very warm in a minute," I tell her and begin working her rosebud open.

She breathes out and relaxes against me, but it still takes some coaxing to get the plug inside, and then a long, quavering moan as the widest part of the bulb stretches her open. Once it's seated in her ass, the jewel winking sweetly between her cheeks, I reward her with the vibrator on her clit, letting her get almost to the brink before I pull back again.

"Jace!" she cries out, frustrated.

"I know, baby," I soothe. "I know." I run a gentling hand over her ass and up her back, petting her. "You're being so good for me right now. So good letting me have what I want."

"Oh God," she says, rolling her face into her forearms. "If I don't come, I'm going to die."

"Then you better be ready for heaven because we aren't done yet."

We play like this for a few more minutes—some buzzing on her clit, some toying with the plug until her entrance is kneaded into pliancy and ready for my cock. She's a moaning, wet mess with slick arousal now coating the outside of her pussy and her inner thighs, and when I see that, I feel like I've been kicked in the stomach.

How am I going to last long enough to make her feel claimed?

Fuck, I'll be lucky if I last another minute.

I climb off the bed and move in front of her so she can see me undress and also so the tempting shine of her wet cunt is out of view. She watches me peel off my shirt and kick off my boots. She watches me unzip and sees my cock push through my fly with wetness all over the blunt tip of it, all for her. Her eyes are huge in the darkness, and her tongue can't seem to stop darting out to lick her lower lip. As if she's desperate to taste me.

I'm light-headed at the thought, and also, Jesus Christ, light-headed that she's here with *me*—dumb, young *me.* She wants me, and I'm going to give her everything in return.

Once she truly knows she's mine, that is.

"Let me see you lube up," she whispers. "I want to see it."

I decide I don't have any objection to this, and I let her watch me as I coat my shaft and the big head with lots of slick lube. I give myself a few more strokes than necessary because it feels so fucking good to squeeze against the ache building deep in my groin.

"I'll go slow," I promise as I mount the bed behind her and remove the plug. "You tell me if you need me to stop."

"Just hurry," she says in that trembling, needy voice that kills me to resist. Resist I must, though, because ideas like *fast* and *rough* don't belong anywhere near *anal*—at least not for the first couple dozen times or so—and I'm determined only to be a caveman in the ways that are fun for us both.

I go slowly, knowing that I'm bigger than the plug, that there's no narrow base at the end to give her relief. I coax my plump crown past her rings, smoothing my hands along her bottom and back as I do, and then I give her a moment to adjust.

"I feel like you've gotten bigger," she says, a touch grumpily, as I slide forward another inch.

"No, baby, you're just small here. Let me in."

She takes a deep breath and forces herself to relent against my intrusion, but it's still a labor of love to get deeper. Still a few hot, urgent moments to get in all the way to the hilt. But then I am, and the sensation of her so tight and hot and smooth around me has all my muscles clenching and rigid against my impending orgasm.

Her first, her first, her first.

I reach for the vibrator and find her clit with it. "You can come now," I say. "Anytime you'd like."

"You don't have to sound so gracious about it," she mumbles, but I can already feel her tightening around me, see her hips trying to chase the delicious rumbles of the toy. I can see the muscles in her thighs trembling and hear the whine building in the back of her throat.

I turn up the vibrator's strength at the same moment I begin thrusting in short, grinding motions to maximize the indirect pressure against her G-spot. Her reaction is instantaneous.

"Oh God, *oh God oh God,*" she whimpers, and the whimpering dies off into a series of sexy-as-fuck, animalistic grunts. "Coming *coming, oh God,* Jace!"

She dissolves. She's shaking, sweating, screaming, her entire body spasming around my cock as she kicks her stockinged feet against the bed and wails her pleasure into her forearm. Each squeeze of her climax clamps down hard on my erection, massaging it, yanking me closer to ejaculation, and I can barely wait for her tremors to subside before I'm flipping her over onto her back and pushing into her ass again.

"Fuck, it's tight," I hiss through my teeth. Her pussy is so wet against my skin as I curl my body over hers to fuck her harder, and I can feel her beaded nipples against my chest and her goose bumps against my own. I meet her gaze and take in her wrecked, dazed expression—hooded eyes and parted lips—and know that I made her that way. I fucked her so thoroughly that she looks like she can't even remember her own name. I gave her what she needed, every filthy minute of it.

"Look at me when I come inside you," I order her. She obeys, her eyes so soft and adoring up at me, even while I'm inside her ass, that I fall in love with her all over again. "Look at me while I take you in a place no one else has. While I claim you."

"Jace," she whispers, and I feel her start to come again. "I'm yours."

Those are the words that push me over the edge. The fist of pleasure that was clenching at the base of my spine finally unclenches, and my orgasm tears through me like a tornado. A hot wave of come spills out of my cock and then another and another, until I'm nothing but jerking, throbbing spurts of ecstasy. Slick and scorching jolts of unraveled man.

I empty my balls inside her and then manage to arrange us so I can collapse on my side, spooning her, with her tucked to my chest and my cock still buried inside her. I want the intimacy of it for another moment longer, just while we come down and catch our breaths. Then I'll untie her and we can clean up.

I stroke along her bare arm, reveling in the silky softness of her skin. A cloud of blond hair is in front of me, giving off some kind of expensive floral scent. Her ass is plump and pressed against my hips, and even as I'm softening, I can feel her body give rhythmic aftershocks.

I think *I'm* the one in heaven now.

"Okay?" I ask.

"Very okay." She sighs in contentment. "I feel very claimed."

"Good. You're mine now. Not his."

She stretches a little, and I slip out of her, wincing at the cool air of the room. This is my cue to untie her, but I have to mourn it a little because elegant Catherine Day looks so fucking good trussed up with her own shredded blouse.

"I was never his, you know," she says as I roll her to her back and start unknotting her shirt. "I agreed to dinner to tell him that nothing was going to happen between us."

I pause my work and search her face. She's telling the truth. "Really?" I ask anyway, needing to hear it.

"Really. I don't want him, Jace, and I think now maybe I never did, even three years ago. He was just there and he made sense, and...I was too lonely not to try."

I wonder if I make sense to her. If I'll ever make sense with my age and my background and my job. I wonder if I'm something she's trying out of loneliness and nothing else.

"Why didn't you tell me this earlier?"

A naughty, kitten-like smile. "I wanted to see what you'd do."

"Dirty girl. And how did he take it?" I ask, finally unlooping the silk and throwing it on the floor. I grab her hands and start massaging them.

She makes a noise of pleasure at my efforts. "Outwardly, fine. But inwardly...I think he was angry and jealous. Bitter, even. It makes me nervous."

Her words cut through me like a knife, and I swallow, forcing myself to focus on doing the best possible job anyone can do massaging a hand.

"And," I say, trying not to sound suddenly suffused with

panic and self-loathing, "is that any different than how I acted tonight?"

"Oh, Jace, of course it is." She sits up, presses her hand against my jaw.

I meet her gaze, miserable. "How?"

"Because I asked."

"Oh."

"And you asked me back. It's that simple, Officer. Now let's take a shower."

CHAPTER ELEVEN

CAT

I wake up in a cloud of happiness so thick that even breathing feels like an act of joy, and in my drowsy state, I can't quite remember why—until I stretch, of course, and my well-abused internal muscles fuss and shout at me.

Oh yes.

Jace.

Last night.

After the anal and a shower, there was more sex—the gentler kind this time, although the orgasms that followed were no more gentle for it. And then we fell asleep snuggled together, spooning as I like to do, with my head pillowed on his big bicep and his legs tangled with mine.

A low male rumble comes from behind me, letting me know that Jace is awake, and I feel him stretch a little and then seek out the back of my neck with his mouth.

"Good morning, baby," he says in a sleepy voice. I shiver at the touch of his lips to my sensitive nape, and he notices—because he's a good cop and notices everything—and then kisses me there again while his hand seeks out a nipple to toy with. "Sleep well?"

"I'll say." I stretch again and roll over into his arms so I can look up into his face. In the fresh morning sunlight and having just woken up, his face is open and boyish, his silver eyes shimmering with molten sin. The place between my thighs tightens at the promise there.

"Shit, you're beautiful," he breathes, ducking his head to kiss my breasts and belly. "So fucking beautiful. I love you so much."

I love you so much.

Love.

A tidal wave of ice-cold water crashes over me, and I'm choking on my own panic. Drowning. Dying.

No. No. He couldn't have said those words. He couldn't have just...*said* them. Like they were no big deal. Like they were beyond self-evident.

Jace lifts his head. "Cat? You okay? You went tense all of a sudden."

"You said you loved me." My voice sounds strangled even to myself.

His handsome face looks so adorably confused, and my heart twists. "Of course I love you," he says, puzzled. "What did you think all that was last night?"

I pull my lower lip between my teeth, distressed.

His expression goes from puzzled to something else. Something wary. Watchful. "I said I was claiming you," he says slowly. "Making you mine. What did you think that meant?"

Excellent question. Even more excellent because didn't I realize last night that I wanted only *him*, that I was falling for him—and doesn't that mean I feel the same way? Doesn't that mean I'm in love with him?

Oh my fucking God, I'm in love with him.

I can't breathe. I can't think. The tidal wave is everywhere, and I'm all cold, flailing panic. I push him away and sit up, needing space, needing...a moment to just fucking think.

"Cat," Jace says, letting me move away but not letting me wriggle out of answering. "Tell me what you *think* this is between us. What we have."

"It's supposed to be just a sex thing," I say, pressing the heels of my hands into my eyes. "Just sex, just fun. That's it."

He takes my wrists and gently tugs my hands down so I have to meet his gaze. "This isn't *just* anything, baby. Not between us. This is real."

I search those gray eyes, so strong and young and sure. "That's what I'm afraid of," I whisper.

His jaw is tight. "Why?"

That he even has to ask reminds me of how new and naïve he is, and the unfairness of it all, the stupid, pointless *waste* of it all cracks me wide open. "Because this can't go anywhere, Jace! It never can! You're just starting, you have your entire life ahead of you, and you are going to find your wife and marry her and have lots of babies, and all of that is still going to be after several years of fucking anything that moves. I'm not going to be the reason you miss out on all that."

If I thought his face was tight before, it's nothing compared to now. I can see the muscles working along the sharp line of his jaw and around the sculpted corners of his mouth, like he's working very hard not to shout. "You don't want me to *miss out*," he repeats.

"Right," I say, even though as I say it, something twists inside me, hard. I know what I just said is true and I know it's necessary, but God, it feels uncommonly depressing to think about. Jace's life after me. Him falling in love and marrying and—

"Fucking other people," he says flatly.

And that.

"So you'd be okay with me sleeping with women who aren't you," he clarifies in a bitter, awful voice. "You'd sleep just fine saying goodbye and knowing I've found a new place for my cock."

I can't help it—I wince. Because I hate it. *I hate it.* I hate the thought of any other woman getting to see the dark line of hair arrowing down from his navel or the way his long eyelashes rest on his cheeks right after he comes. I loathe the thought of anyone else knowing the flex and clench of his ass as he fucks...or the hard lengths of his thighs straining as he gets ridden...or the rough, male authority of those hands that grab and hold and squeeze as he makes love.

Most of all, I hate the thought of someone else using his bicep as a pillow. Knowing the warm fan of his breath in their hair. Getting to wake up to sleepy gray eyes already blazing with possession.

And I can't meet those gray eyes now as I think about all this.

Hating it doesn't change anything, I remind myself. He's still too young. He's still a cop. This is all still so wrong.

Jace catches my chin with his fingers and forces me to look at him. "Is it really such a huge thing? Our ages? Because it's not to me, and if anyone says anything to you about it, I'll tell them as much." His gaze darkens. "Or more."

The noise that comes out of my mouth is a sour, scoffing noise that I'd ordinarily be appalled at making. "What are you going to do, Jace? Beat the shit out of every person who calls me a cougar?"

He starts to object at the word, but I go on. "Are you going to shake up every person who stares at us, wondering if I'm your older sister or an aunt—or worse, your mother? Walk around with a sandwich board telling people to fuck off?"

His eyes are narrowed now, and I feel the heat of that cop gaze scrutinizing me, and I hate it. I hate that he's examining me while I'm shredded with fear and messy with feelings I didn't ask for. Catherine Day isn't supposed to be shredded or messy—I'm always contained and cool. Icy, just like the rest of the department says I am. And not being icy when I most need to be is infuriating.

I toss my head away from Jace's fingers like an agitated filly. "And what are you going to say to yourself, Jace? In a year? In five? In twenty? When you've thrown away your life chasing something ridiculous instead of living it the way you should?"

I'm pinned to the bed before I can blink, two hundred pounds of pissed-off cop looming over me and pressing my body into the mattress. "You are *not* ridiculous," Jace growls. "And you're not allowed to say that shit about yourself. Not while I'm around. Got it?"

Despite everything, the insane chemistry between us is setting my skin aflame. I can feel my nipples pebble between us, his cock go rigid and hot in the notch between my legs, both our hearts hammering hard against our chests as if they're trying to trade places. I want him to kiss me. I want him to eat my mouth like he's starving and then fuck me screaming into the bed.

Jace looks like he very much wants the same, his arms trembling where he holds himself above me and his eyes dropping to my mouth like he can't decide whether he wants to kiss me or shove his cock down my throat.

I moan, and his control breaks—for a single instant. He drops his mouth onto mine for a crashing, ragged kiss, but before I can even begin to kiss him back, he's gone. He's off the bed, staring at me, naked, his denied erection dark and bobbing between his legs. He ignores it and bites out, "We're not going to do that."

"Do what?"

"Fuck the fight away," he says shortly. "That's not going to help anything."

"Because it can't be helped, Jace."

He ducks his head, muscles popping in his jaw, but he doesn't argue my point.

Which leaves me feeling a little stung, although I'm not even sure why, given that I started this fight. And I'm not even sure *what* I feel anymore, actually, just that it's a million things at once. Like maybe a secret part of my mind was hoping he'd keep trying to convince me that we could overcome this.

"I can't help my age, Cat," he finally says.

"I know," I say. "But it's not just that."

"Oh," he says, his posture stiffening even more. "That's

right. The badge."

I blink, and in that blink, I see my dead fiancé's sightless stare and an ocean of blood.

I sigh. "Yes."

"You're a cop too," he says. Accuses.

"Exactly." I get to my feet now as well, which maybe is a mistake because it only serves to highlight how much taller he is, but I don't care. "I already carry all the fear and the trauma for myself. I can't carry it for another person. I can't wait up every night wondering if this will be the night you don't come home. I can't be the one waiting on that phone call, Jace. I just...can't."

"Are you saying you don't worry now?" he asks, taking a step forward. "Are you saying because it's only been a few weeks, because we haven't put labels on anything, you wouldn't give a shit if I lived or died?"

My mouth drops open. *Of course not,* I want to sputter, but he keeps going.

"Because maybe you feel that way, but if you don't think I'm already in so deep that I wouldn't be in fucking agony if you were hurt, then think again."

I'm staring up at him—defensive and confused—and whatever he sees in my face is not the right answer because he reaches down for his clothes and starts yanking them on in jerky, vicious motions that make me suddenly desperate to take back everything I've just said.

"Jesus, Cat," he mutters, pulling his T-shirt over his head. "You can't freeze out everything, you know. And I'll be damned if I'll let you do it to me."

"Where are you going?" I ask as he shoves his feet in his boots. "You can stay. We can...talk."

He shoots me a dark look. "If I stay, we're not going to talk."

"I'm okay with that," I whisper.

He gives a cheerless laugh. "Of course you are. I'm good enough to fuck, but that's it, right?"

Irritation stabs through me, fast and sharp. "I never said that."

"You don't have to." He gets to the doorway, swiping his keys and wallet off the dresser and turning to face me. The morning sunlight pouring in from the living room outlines his hewn, perfect form in hazy gold. "Here's what I can't figure out," he says with a glare that raises the hairs along my arms. "How can you say you're afraid of having your heart broken if you can't even admit you have a heart at all?"

It's a fair question, and it lands with a punch. I stagger backward a step and sit heavily on my bed, unable to meet his eyes.

And he leaves without another word. He leaves me naked and alone and searching for an answer to a question I should have asked myself the moment we met.

♦♦♦♦

It's the weekend, and since Jace is on my mini–task force of two, he has the weekend off as well. But he doesn't call that night or the next day. He doesn't text or stop by.

I don't reach out either.

Instead, I catch up on work email and a few other cases

I've had to shelve while I've focused on the burglaries. I go grocery shopping. I do a yoga class. I call my parents, who've retired in France, and we catch up on the last couple of weeks. They beg me to come out and stay a month. They drop hints about how much fun their little farmhouse and pond would be for children.

I usually dodge the hints easily enough, but this time, my voice catches when I say I haven't been really dating anyone.

"Catherine?" Mom asks. "*Is* there someone?"

I don't know how to answer that. "Sort of," I hedge. "It's complicated."

"What isn't?" Mom laughs. "I've been married to your father for forty-one years, and it's still complicated. Is it another police officer?"

"It is."

"You don't sound happy about it."

I sigh. "We fought yesterday."

Mom takes a minute to reply to that, and when she does, she says, "You know, sometimes your father and I worry about how we raised you. The...impressions...we might have left, without meaning to, and I just worry that it's made things harder for you now that you're grown."

"You're going to have to be less vague," I tell her, "because I don't understand." And I mean it. My parents were the ideal parents. One a judge, one a doctor. They doted on me, their only child, and while there were certain expectations of etiquette and demeanor required of me, I never doubted their love. Or their respect, once I reached adulthood.

"I'm afraid we've raised you to be, well, *picky*," she says carefully.

"Oh, Mom."

"We really did adore Frazer," she forges on quickly, "but maybe your father and I didn't tell you enough that we didn't mind that he was, you know, *poor*." She whispers this last word as if it's not a word for polite company, and I lean my head against the doorway I'm standing in.

"Mom."

"We're so proud of what you do and that you do it for not very much money. It's so honorable, and we would extend the same perception to any police officer you wanted to date."

I'm suddenly and fiercely grateful I never told them about Kenneth, because I know with a deep, regretful certainty that dating Kenneth wouldn't have required this conversation. They would have been overjoyed with Kenneth's background and career in law, especially my retired judge of a father, and we never would have had this talk about them *not minding* someone I loved.

It's both exasperating and sweet, I suppose, that Mom feels these things must be said to me now. Exasperating because, generally, when someone goes out of their way to tell you they don't mind something, it's indicative that they *do* mind, on some level. And sweet because I can tell she means well, in her own privileged way.

"That's thoughtful of you," I say because I'm truly not sure how to respond.

"I know," Mom says with benign obliviousness. And then she adds, "And we just really, really want to have some grandchildren before we die!"

I manufacture an excuse to get off the phone very quickly

after that, but her words find their mark. Not because her guilt finds any real home in me but because her words echo the fleeting, forbidden fantasies that have been chasing through my own mind. Feeling my belly swell with Jace's baby. Watching his big, strong hands cradle our child. Seeing him play on the floor and roughhouse and carry our child on his shoulders.

Fantasies that would rob him of his youth and the rest of his life.

Fantasies that can never come true.

♦♦♦♦

Monday morning finds me at my desk two hours earlier than normal.

Without Jace laid out behind me in a wall of warm male, I find it hard to sleep, and then I also find myself intensely irritated because I shouldn't miss him so damn much after such a short time. After repeatedly telling myself nothing can ever come of our ill-advised liaison. After doing my goddamn best to guard my heart.

But I do miss him. I do.

After tossing and turning and barely skimming under the surface of consciousness into bleak dreams, I finally gave up and decided to start the day. So here I am, poring back over the license plate data from the last burglary. Last week, I had Jace run the plates through our system to see if anything came back flagged as linked to a criminal record, and we got a few hits. All dead ends.

Now I'm back to the beginning, narrowing the list down to the plates caught in the hour before the alarm was triggered and then seeing if I can find any patterns. It stands to reason that any burglar worth their salt would have done reconnaissance before—at least driven by once or twice—so I go back to the larger data pool to see if I can find any matches.

Ah, the glory of detective work. Spreadsheet-driven analysis and data tabulation. No wonder there's so many TV shows about us.

After getting a fresh mug of hot water for tea—tea that I get endless taunting for drinking in a station full of coffee addicts—I pull up emails from the different office managers listing the plates of employee cars so I can eliminate them from any potential patterns I find. I highlight all of those and then cross-reference them with information from the burglary sites.

I find something.

I roll out my shoulders and take a sip of tea as I consider the screen, and then I pull up our informational system and run a plate through. Since it's a cop system, it takes a long minute to load, and I click back to the spreadsheet while it searches, tapping my fingers against my lips.

The same plate number pops up at four of the five burglaries within an hour of the alarms being triggered. And at scene number five? The car passed through the closest intersection at 7:48 that morning and didn't pass back through until 10:23 at night. Three minutes after the alarm had been triggered.

Drywall, I think. *The stupid drywall.*

I click back to the database to see the car is registered to a woman in her late forties named Debbie Pisani.

I scribble a quick note to Jace about where I'm going, grab the keys to a squad car, and head out the door, calling a patrol captain as I go.

CHAPTER TWELVE

JACE

I nearly jerk my dick raw that weekend, being away from Cat. Three weeks of her in my bed and I've turned into something insatiable and ravenous. I've always had a healthy appetite before, but now with Cat, my need to fuck has exploded into a ceaseless, throbbing ache. An ache only she can ease, and she's not here to do it.

I could call. I know I could. I could show up at her doorstep right now, and she'd let me inside and we'd fuck until this awful thing between us tucked its tail and hid. We could lose ourselves and our hurt in each other's bodies, and maybe things would go back to how they were.

But I don't want that.

I don't want things to be how they were. I want *more*, and I'm not going to cheat us out of something better simply because a day and a half without Cat is agony.

No.

I love her. I need her forever. And I know I'm going to need every tool in the box to woo her away from these superstitions about age and occupation.

The most important tool: time.

Time for both of us to cool down. To miss each other. Time for the argument to recede enough that we can see all the unspoken fears underneath the words we said to each other.

So I settled for my hand as my body demanded its woman, and I made plans. Of what to say, what proofs to give, of when I'd concede her points and when I'd kiss the arguments right off her perfect mouth. We just have to get through work today, and then I'll take her home and tell her about my love over and over again until she realizes that love is strong enough to swallow up everything else. What are some years between us when I love her so much? What is a *job*? Nothing at all.

But she's not at her desk when I get there, even though I'm easily fifteen minutes early. I set down the cup of tea and donut I got for her—despite all the silk blouses and high school dressage trophies, Cat likes donuts just as much as any other cop, although she prefers the gourmet honey-and-sea-salt-type flavors to the glazed ones we usually have at the station—and then read over the note she left by her desk.

Ran out to reinterview Gia Pisani. Back by lunch.

I'm reading it over a second and third time when the phone at her desk rings. I answer it, in case it's her.

"Sutton."

"Um, hi," comes a hesitant voice. "This is Shelley Abadinksy, from the Mastin Cancer Center office? I'm calling for Detective Day?"

"She's away from her desk at the moment," I say, glancing at her note. Conclusions are fitting together in my mind, and there's a sharp bite of worry in my chest. The itch to go find her is difficult to think through. "I'm one of the officers assisting her on the case. I can take a message and make sure she gets it."

"Sure," Shelley says, sounding relieved. "And actually you might be able to help me anyway. I had our office manager, Gia Pisani, send in an updated inventory of all the missing items, but I just realized we might have to contact some federal authority, and I thought maybe Detective Day would know which one."

I'm standing and my body is already angled toward the cubicle opening, I'm that desperate to get to Cat right now. So I say hurriedly, "No need to report the televisions to anybody federal, ma'am. We'll handle it all here at HGPD," and make to hang up.

"Oh, I'm not talking about the televisions," she says, surprised. "Did Gia not tell you? Our cobalt therapy machine has been damaged, and the cobalt inside was stolen."

"Cobalt?"

"Nuclear material? It's used for radiation therapy."

Cobalt. It rings a bell from my army days, and my already tight hand practically cracks the phone receiver in half.

Cobalt. It's used for radiation therapy...*and dirty bombs*.

"And you didn't notice it was missing until now?"

She sounds defensive when she answers. "Look, we just refitted a new therapy room with a LINAC machine, so we haven't used the cobalt machine in over a month. It was scheduled to be removed next week. I went in there Friday to take a few measurements for the disposal company. That's when I noticed it had been pried open."

And Gia Pisani is the office manager. Cat is interviewing her right now.

Things come together in a horrible rush.

"And I just wasn't sure if *we* needed to contact someone like the Nuclear Regulatory Commission or if you did that," she goes, oblivious to the fact that I'm splitting apart with panic on my end.

"Shelley, I'm going to call you back, but I have to go right now."

"Okay, but—"

"We didn't know about the nuclear material," I tell her, already reaching up to click on my radio. "And I have to tell a lot of people about it right now so no one gets hurt."

"Oh," she says faintly, the gravity of it finally seeming to sink in. "Oh, of course. I should have—yes, of course."

"Goodbye, ma'am." And then I'm hanging up the phone and calling for a captain on the radio.

♦♦♦♦

"Day's got two uniforms with her," Captain Kim tells me as I'm speeding south to the medical office. "More are on the way."

"And the NRC?"

"Notified." A pause. "And the KBI and the FBI."

"Is she with Pisani now?"

"They're in the staff breakroom at the back of the building. The uniforms are just outside the door. Pisani doesn't know they're there. Everything's under control, Sutton."

Funny how hard that is to believe when the woman I love is alone with a criminal who is apparently selling nuclear material on the black market. I click off the radio and focus on driving, pushing the low-profile detective car to its limits. It roars into the parking lot before any of the supervisors arrive, which is good. I don't need them forbidding me from going in, because I'm going in no matter what.

I park and push my way into the building. There's an unfamiliar woman at the desk who looks puzzled at my appearance, so I assume she doesn't know about the other cops in the building.

"Where's your staff room?" I ask through gritted teeth, trying to keep my voice low.

"Back by the lab," she says, still puzzled. "First left. Hey, are you with that one lady—"

I don't stay to chat. I move down the hallway as quick as I can, pressing the hood of my holster down and forward in preparation for drawing my weapon. I pray I don't have to, because if I have to, it means Cat's in danger...

I round the corner and see a door marked *Employees Only*. Taking a risk, I open it with wary, slow caution, making sure I can slide into the restricted area without being seen or creating any noise. After I'm in, I close the door with a barely audible *click* and enter a fluorescent-lit hallway to see two patrol officers outside a windowed room. One of them puts a finger to her lips, indicating I need to be silent, and I creep up to join them.

Through the window of the staff room, I see Cat sitting across a cheap table from Gia Pisani, two disposable cups of coffee between them. Gia is agitated but trying to hide it under a veneer of friendly confusion.

Cat is unreadable—save for the occasional twitch of her lips as Gia talks. The Ice Queen's signature cool amusement. It seems to piss Gia off.

For a moment, I relax. It's just an interview in a forgettably bland staff room—a tense interview, maybe, but nothing more. No weapons, no open containers of nuclear waste, no anonymous men here to protect their supply. Cat doesn't know about the nuclear material yet, which means she won't question Pisani about it, which means the interview probably won't escalate into—

Gia stands abruptly, her chair knocking back behind her, her cheeks glowing as she says something heated to Cat.

Cat merely crosses her arms and arches a perfect brow, as if to make the point that the young woman is embarrassing herself with this outburst. Like most cops, Cat has the gift of complete reticence—that is, refraining from reacting to another person until she's good and ready—and her lack of response only provokes Gia to say more. Which was probably Cat's intention the entire time.

Hardly any sound makes it through the window, and at this angle, it's hard to attempt any kind of interpretation to what Gia says, but Cat tilts her head and murmurs something in an unperturbed tone.

Gia blanches, and I know whatever Cat said hit home. Hard.

She's so fucking good at this.

Weird how I *feel* that thought in the pit of my stomach—

not with lust but with fear.

Because she's so good, she's more than good—she's sharply perceptive, intelligent beyond measure, fierce as hell, and that's not even taking into account all that sophistication and beauty. She's so far out of my league that we've never even played on the same field, and with a sudden, gripping terror, I wonder if *that* was what our fight was about. If she's not truly worried about our age difference or my job, but if she's trying to let me down easy because I'm not good enough for her.

And shit—she'd be right. I'm not.

I have to glance down to take a breath—a big, deep one to try to stave off panic I've never known before, and right at that moment, something happens that blows even that panic right out of the water. Gia shrieks something and, in a clumsy but quick movement, fumbles a gun from behind her back where it was tucked in her waistband.

She aims it right at Cat.

I'm moving before I can think, my gun out and my shoulder ramming the flimsy interior door open, and it's like all sound and feeling are gone, all extraneous sensation. There's only the gun in my hand and the palpable presence of the woman I love who's about to die.

She can't die.

Oh God. She can't die.

Reality comes back in with a vicious, adrenaline-laced flood.

The explosion of me through the door draws Gia's attention, and I hear myself yell for her to drop her weapon. I hear the two other cops behind me shouting for Gia to get on the ground.

Cat says something in a low, soothing tone as she gets to her feet and gracefully gestures for everyone to lower their weapons, and for a moment I think Gia is going to do it. I think she's going to drop her gun and give up this pointless resistance.

But then the officer behind me speaks again, his voice jangling with sheer human panic, and it jars Gia free from thoughts of surrender.

She swings the gun.

She shoots.

And pain, big and stark, swallows me whole.

Then darkness.

CHAPTER THIRTEEN

CAT

I've died. I've died and I've gone to hell.

And I'm not even the one who was shot.

A cup of coffee appears in my vision. Black, slightly oily, tiny bubbles rimming the edge of the liquid where it sloshed gently against the paper cup. I take it, although the idea of drinking or eating anything while my stomach is still twisted up into my throat is laughable. I don't bother to look over as Russo settles next to me, her own cup of coffee in hand.

"How is he?" she asks.

"Stable, last I heard. The bullet caught an artery in his arm and he lost a lot of—" My voice catches, and I suck in a breath, forcing myself to face tonight's events with the usual blunt, cold honesty I face everything else with. "He lost a lot of blood," I manage after a moment. "They closed the wound and did a transfusion, and he's recovering now. I should be able to see him soon."

Russo reaches out, touches my hand with her rough, unmanicured fingers. I know she sees the dried blood still trapped along the lines of my cuticles. "You saved his life," she says quietly.

"Maybe," I say, because at no point during those frantic, bloody moments after the gun went off did I allow myself to hope. At no point when I stanched his wound with my bare hands, the scene cruelly overlaid with my memories of trying to save Frazer, did I let myself believe it could end any differently.

Instead, I felt his hot, wet blood against my skin, sticky and slick all at once, and I thought *it's happening again.*

It's happening.

Again.

The uniforms cuffed Gia while she was frozen in horror at what she'd done—we arrested her without any one of us firing a weapon or using any kind of force. Good police work any way you slice it, and the paramedics were a credit to the city. They arrived as fast as humanly possible and took charge of Jace's life with expert competence.

Someone had to peel me away while they worked. Another paramedic? Captain Kim, maybe? But I was allowed to ride in the ambulance with him. Allowed to hold the hand on his good arm while I frantically searched for all the prayers from my Catholic upbringing.

I could only remember fragments, and finally my thoughts disintegrated into vague, broken pleas as the ambulance raced to the hospital.

Please don't let him die.

Please.

Don't let him die.

"There was nothing else you could have done," Russo points out in the here and now. "The other officers told me what happened. You had the interview under control, and from what it sounds like, you might have been able to talk her down even without Sutton crashing in."

"I should have searched her first," I murmur.

"You wouldn't have been able to—not without cause—and what you had on her going into the interview would have been pretty weak grounds for a body search from a court's perspective."

She's right, and I know she's right, and it's almost worse that way. It's almost worse to know I did everything right and *still.*

Still.

I take a drink of the coffee. Not because I like it or because I need time to think, but just because it's something to do. Some new input that isn't self-recrimination and terror and misery.

"He did what Frazer did," I say after a minute and mostly out of nowhere.

"Yeah," Russo sighs. "I know."

"Why do they do that?"

Russo gives a dry laugh. "Who? Cops? Men? Men who are in love with you?"

I don't want to answer that, and I can't anyway.

"I know he's in love, Day," Russo adds gently. "All anyone has to do is look at him and know he's gone for you."

"He's young," I say, trying to sound dismissive. It only comes out as sad. "He doesn't know what he wants."

"I disagree," Russo says. "I think you're the one who doesn't know what she wants."

"He did what Frazer did," I repeat softly, and she gives me a rueful look.

"Is that so unforgivable?"

I look down at my fingers, still stained with Jace's blood. "It might be."

♦♦♦♦

An hour later, with Russo gone and Jace's family camped all around me, a nurse comes in to say we can go in to see him—but we can't go all at once.

I'm desperate to get to him, desperate to trace his lips with my fingers and reassure myself that they're still warm. Anxious to see the rise and fall of his chest and know he's here. Still here. Still alive.

But Jace's parents are here, and they have the right to go first. I lace my fingers around the cup of tepid coffee and give Jace's mother a look I hope she'll interpret as a signal that I won't protest her going first...no matter how much I want to.

She walks up to me. "You're Cat Day?" she asks. Her voice is fractured from crying, and tear tracks have dried in streaks along her cheeks. She's very pretty—gray-eyed and full-lipped like Jace, and as tall and broad as he is too.

"I am," I say quietly. "Please, you go in first."

She gives me a watery smile. "Jace told us about you," she says, tucking a gray-salted lock of hair behind her ear. "That you two were dating, and he couldn't wait—" Her chin trembles. "He couldn't wait for us to meet."

Jace told his mother about me? Wanted us to meet? My heart flips over at the discovery, at the proof that his declarations weren't just the lust-fueled blurtings I'd suspected. That he not only wanted more with me but was actively laying the foundation for more.

Telling his parents. Wanting me to meet them.

The same things my illicit fantasies have been showing me for the last three weeks: a real life together.

My flattered joy is tempered with something unpleasant. I look up at his mother and realize she can't be more than ten years older than me. I realize she's looking down at me and seeing...

Seeing what?

A predator? A peer?

Both options are depressing.

"What you must think of me," I manage with a weak smile, and she shakes her head.

She reaches out and touches my shoulder. Not as a gesture of comfort but to draw my attention. I look at her hands, rough and calloused like Russo's, and remember that she was a firefighter. That her son's bravery and dedication to hard work comes from her.

She's touching stiffened patches of garnet splattered on my blouse. There's dried blood all over me; I look like I've emerged from some kind of abattoir.

"I think you're a hero," she pronounces. "You saved his life."

And then she and her husband follow the nurse into the ICU.

♦♦♦♦

It's another hour before they leave, and finally I get to go in.

Jace is still unconscious, his face pale and his huge frame

dwarfed by the massive mechanical bed, and I cover my mouth with my hand so my unhappy gasp doesn't wake him. As if anything could wake him up after all that blood loss and morphine.

There's a chair pulled up beside his bed, but I ignore it, dropping my things on the floor and crawling right into bed with him, careful not to tug on any cords or tubes as I do. He's warm but not as warm as I'm used to, and I'm just as cold as I press my body along his and lay my head on his good shoulder.

"Jace," I mumble. "Why? Why are we here?"

Tears are leaking now—the fast, uncontrollable kind and the first I've cried since Gia fired that gun. "I love you," I finally admit, hating myself that I never told him before. That I never told him when it mattered. "I love you, and it scares me. It scares me because you love me back and you love me back so much that you'd get yourself killed trying to protect me."

Just like Frazer.

Beneath my cheek, I feel Jace's steady if shallow breathing. All around us, various machines and monitors beep and glow with reassuring consistency, as if to say *he's doing okay, he's doing okay*.

But how can I ever be reassured of his safety ever again? After I've been spattered with coppery, vibrant blood as I begged and begged him to stay alive?

Maybe he didn't die today, but he came close enough to prove every point I've ever made about us. He is blessed enough to live and have this second chance, and surely he doesn't want to waste it on a woman so much older than him. Surely he deserves more tomcat years before he even has to think about settling down.

And most importantly...

He's too young and he's too heroic.

I've loved those young heroes before. I know what happens. I know how it ends.

I cry for a long time into his big, muscled shoulder, leaving streaks of mascara on his hospital gown. I slide my hand over his chest to feel the thump of his heart, and I listen to the machines, and I tell him, "I love you, I love you, I love you."

And before I leave, I kiss his stubbled jaw and say, "And I'm so fucking sorry for what I have to do."

CHAPTER FOURTEEN

JACE

I'm too dizzy to open my eyes.

Sounds bleed through the haze of strange dreams—sounds I don't recognize—and I can't open my eyes to see what they are because the world is spinning, spinning, spinning.

I smell something familiar. A delicate, French perfume, and the smell conjures a face in my mind.

Cat...

But before I can manage to speak her name, heavy, drugged unconsciousness pulls at me, the sounds receding as I disappear back into the spinning dark.

♦♦♦♦

When I wake again, the dizziness isn't so bad, but Cat's scent has disappeared into a miasma of cleaning chemicals and fast food. I manage to pry open my bleary eyes to find my parents sitting next to me, McDonald's cups in hands, talking in low tones about replacing the fence in their backyard.

"Mom?" I rasp.

"Oh!" she says, setting her cup down and rushing to lean

over me. "Oh God, Jace, you're awake!"

She sounds happy and sad all at once, and even in my groggy state of mind, I can see the drawn lines around her mouth and eyes, the ashen cast to her face. Whatever I've been through, she's suffered more watching me go through it. My dad joins her on the other side of the bed, taking my hand.

I'm so glad to see them, although the reasons why are hazy...

"Where's Cat?" I whisper. "She was here, I know she was..."

Mom and Dad exchange a look over me. Mom's look distinctly says *I told you so.*

"She's been here constantly," Mom says as she looks back at me. "We sent her home today to get a change of clothes and a nap. She hasn't been taking care of herself since you came in."

I close my eyes, pained that Cat has been suffering but hopeful too—hopeful that if she's been here and had to be forced to leave that it means something for us. For our future.

"How long?" I ask. My voice is dry and raspy. "How long have I been here?"

"Three days," Dad says. "The first day was the hardest—"

His voice cracks, and he clears his throat in a manly sort of way. "You got moved down from the ICU yesterday. They say you're in good shape—no sign of infection so far. They'll be in to assess potential nerve damage later."

Infection.

Damage.

The haze clears a bit around what I'm feeling in my body—like my right arm is on fire—and *why* I'm feeling it. Gia's face, florid and angry, her hand shaking around the gun so hard that she could barely keep it still.

Cat, slender and cool, eyebrow arched as she stared down the barrel without so much as flinching.

The barb of real, primal terror that lodged in my heart when I realized Cat was about to die. I've never felt fear like that. Not even in Afghanistan.

Funnily enough, I was also never actually wounded in Afghanistan. It was here, on these mean suburban streets, by a Vassar grad with a flair for supplying terrorists with rare metals. Who would've guessed?

With my parents' help, I sit up and manage to chew some ice chips, and then I fall back asleep, the seductive pull of the pain medicine too strong to resist. I don't dream much, but what I do dream is strange and warped and distressing. And always, always about Cat.

When I wake up again, it's dark outside the window and the nearby highway is mostly drained of traffic. The lights in the room are dimmed, and a television is playing a rerun of a sitcom I normally hate. But I'm too tired and out of it to bother trying to find a way to change the channel.

Most importantly, there's someone in bed with me. Someone warm and sweet-smelling. My arm wraps around her instinctively, pressing her tight against me as my heart squeezes in a familiar, achy way.

The monitor next to me reflects that, and Cat shoots upright in alarm.

"Jace," she says urgently, searching my face. "Are you okay?"

"Yes," I murmur. "Just awake. Just holding you."

The panic recedes from her expression slowly. "Does your arm hurt? Do you need the nurse?"

"Cat," I say, reaching for her again. "I only need you."

With a huff of disbelief, she nestles back into me, and I savor the feeling of her close to me. My body gives a faint pulse of aroused response—muffled by the pain meds—and I ignore it for now, simply enjoying the contact. Enjoying the weight of her against me and the spill of her hair, messy and tousled as it hardly ever is, cascading over my shoulder. She's in something surprisingly casual too—jeans torn at the knees and cuffed at the ankles—and an old army shirt that I left at her house once.

For some reason, seeing her in my shirt makes me want to cry. I fight off the urge by burying my face in her hair and breathing her in.

She's here.

She's safe.

I kept her safe.

♦ ♦ ♦ ♦

A few more days pass like this. Russo comes by and tells me I'm on medical leave until I'm cleared by the doctor to come back to light duty. Cat comes in at night, after my parents leave and always wearing my shirts, and snuggles in the bed with me, much to the nurses' amusement. She doesn't say much, which begins to worry me, and every time I bring up the case or my injury, she shuts down completely.

I'm not sure what to do about it. I want her to know how happy I am she's safe. How few fucks I give about getting shot when it means that she's here now, unharmed and whole. Even if I have lingering impairment in my arm that means I can't wear the badge anymore...

Worth. It.

I'd do it again and again if it meant Cat left that staff room alive.

But the more I try to tell her that, the more closed off she gets. I'm desperate to get out of this hospital bed and into a real bed with her so we can extinguish all this pent-up frustration and fear in a frenzy of touch and sweat. If I could just get her underneath me...

She's in bed with me now. The lights are dimmed and the nurse just checked on me, giving me a conspiratorial wink when she shut the door, and I know we have at least an hour or more before she returns. Without giving myself time to doubt the wisdom of this, I tuck Cat close to my side and roll us so that she's underneath me and I'm covering my body with hers. I have to grit my teeth a bit as I settle my weight on my injured arm along with my good one, but the stitches hold and the Demerol blunts the worst of the bite.

"Jace!" Cat says breathlessly, blinking over at the door and then to my injured arm. "You'll hurt yourself. You'll—"

I cut her off with a fierce, hard kiss—the first real one I've been able to give her since the shooting. I silently thank God that I've been able to walk around the past two days and shower and brush my teeth and all that, because I don't have to hold back. I lick at her lips until she parts them for me, and then I lick inside her mouth, tasting her and teasing her until her wary body begins to melt under mine. Until she's moaning and her hands wander to the back of my hospital gown to clutch at my ass.

"The only way I'll hurt," I breathe against her lips, "is if you don't let me taste you right now."

"Taste me? But—"

It's too late. I'm already working my way down her body, careful of my IV and monitor wires, and rucking up her borrowed T-shirt to kiss around her navel as I unbutton her jeans.

"You can't," she says, "you can't, but oh God, you are, *you are...*"

I yank the jeans down past her cunt, ignoring the sharp pain in my arm as I shove the denim to her knees and expose her silk-clad mound to my stare. The silk goes down to her knees too, and then I push her legs up to her chest so that she's available to my mouth.

I lick her slit, and the sweet, earthy flavor explodes on my tongue. She cries out at the same time my heart monitor pings its alarm.

"Shh," I pant, "or the nurse might come in."

She presses the back of her hand to her mouth and turns her head to the side, as if that's going to make my onslaught any easier to bear. I highly doubt that, since it's been nearly a week since I've eaten her pussy and I'm hungry as hell.

It's hard work to service her properly, with her legs bound together by her jeans and her knees shoved up to her chest, and with my body hanging off the bottom of the bed and my ass hanging out of my gown.

But I don't care—it's like heaven to me. Burying my face, getting my lips and chin wet, seeking out her swollen little clit with my tongue and stroking it. Lapping at her entrance like it's the only real medicine I need.

I have to force myself to breathe, to be calm, because I know there's only so much I can push that heart monitor before the nurse feels compelled to check on me, no matter how much she wants to be my wingwoman.

But it's nearly impossible to slow it down. I can't keep my heart from pounding in anticipation. Can't keep blood from going right to the throbbing weight between my legs.

Although judging from the way my balls have drawn up tight to my body, I'm guessing I won't be making the heart monitor go off for long. After so many days without her, her taste alone is enough to send me to the edge. And then she comes against my tongue with a muffled cry, her sweet little well contracting in rhythmic flutters, her hand reaching around and twisting in my hair to keep my mouth right where she needs it.

I can't last.

With a quick move that has my arm screaming, I'm back on the bed and rolling her to her side as I get behind her. I manage to plunge in right at the end of her orgasm, and I have to clap my hand over her mouth as she starts coming all over again at the fresh invasion.

It only takes three thrusts and the feeling of her moaning against my palm before I'm there, emptying everything I have inside her, pumping her full of a week's worth of need, and all to the beeping consternation of the heart monitor. Its insistent tones underscore my final few thrusts as I give Cat every last drop of what I have, and then it finally begins to settle down as I slide out of her and pull her snug against me.

We're both wet and messy and her pants are still around her legs, but I don't want to move. I just want to hold her tight and relish the sensation of having her here and close and safe.

My woman.

Mine.

Cat wriggles free, though, not saying anything as she reaches for a tissue to clean up. Not meeting my eyes as she pulls up her panties and jeans.

A slow curl of unease blooms in my chest. "Cat? Baby?"

She doesn't answer at first, still buttoning herself and smoothing back her hair, until finally and with a long swallow, she meets my stare.

Oh God.

I don't know what's happening or why, and I don't know what she's about to say—but I'm certain she's about to leave me. There's something about the hollow pain in her gaze and the unhappiness around the lines of her plush mouth...something about her posture that looks defensive and determined all at once.

"Cat," I say again, sitting up. The heart monitor, which was calming down, starts beeping faster. "Don't do this. Don't do this to me."

She takes a breath, like she's steeling herself. "Jace."

"No." The beeping makes it hard to think, but the more frantic I feel, the faster it gets. "No, Cat. I don't know what you're thinking, but *no*."

"I held off doing this," she whispers. "I thought I'd wait until you woke up...and then I thought I'd wait until you were discharged, but I was just fooling myself because I don't want to leave..."

"Then why do it?" I demand. "Why put us through this when I love you?"

She lifts her eyes to the ceiling, ignoring my plea. "I thought you were going to die. I felt your blood on my hands, and there was so much, and I thought how can anyone lose this much blood and still—" She pauses, steadies her voice. "I can't go through that again. I used to think I couldn't go through it for anyone after Frazer, but it's *you*... I can't go through it with *you*. I love you too damn much."

I'm off the bed in an instant, but my IV and monitor wires mean I can't get close to her. I want to rip them all off and go and gather her into my arms. Crush her against my chest and kiss her hair until she stops this madness.

"If you love me," I try to reason with her, "then everything else will work out." I reach out my hand, knowing that I must look ridiculous in my bare feet and my hospital gown, but I don't even care. I just want her to come closer. I just want her to stay.

"No," she says, and her chin is trembling. She still won't look at me. "I wish that were true, I really do, but loving each other doesn't erase who we are. You'll always be in danger—"

"I'll stop," I interrupt her. "I'll quit. If quitting is what it takes, I'd do it in a heartbeat for you."

"No!" she cries. "That's not what I want at all! I don't want you to change who you are or what you love to do."

"It's just a *job*, Cat. I can find another one."

"Can you?" she whispers. "Can you tell me you don't miss the action from when you were deployed? Can you really tell me you won't be bored doing something else, something safe?"

I open my mouth.

Close it.

I can't lie to her.

"And you're a hero, Jace," she adds, blinking fast at the ceiling. "You're a good cop. We need more of those. *I* need more of those, because I'm not planning on giving up this job either, and I want cops like you by my side. I just can't *love* them."

"It's too late for that," I say roughly. "You already do."

She finally meets my eyes, and what I see there shreds me. Those aren't the eyes of someone about to fall on a sword—they are the eyes of someone who's already fallen.

"I love you enough to know that I'll ruin your life," she says in a broken voice. "Thirteen years is too big of a hurdle. You might think it's not now, but what about in twenty years? When I'm close to sixty and you're still in your forties? When you've felt forced into deciding whether or not to have children because it's not going to be possible for me to do it much longer? You deserve to spend your years free of all that. Free of responsibility until you *choose* it."

"I'm choosing it now," I rumble, trying to pull closer and feeling the IV in my hand protest. "Why is that so hard to believe? I don't want to spend those years being 'free.' I don't want to spend any years without you at all."

"It's been three weeks," she says. "It all feels real now, but it's not, Jace. It can't be."

"It *is*."

Goddammit, it is.

"I'm sorry I couldn't let you go sooner," she whispers. "It was selfish of me to wait, to want to be with you one last time..."

She takes a step back, and I know if she walks out that door, I'll lose her forever. It really will be the end. I make to yank off the monitor wires, and her eyes flare in panic.

"Stop it," she pleads, and I don't care. I'm not letting her leave. I'm not letting her finish us when I know she loves me, when I love her, when she's mine.

I tear them off my chest, not even feeling the sting, and then I start on my IV, trying to peel back the clear bandage they put on top.

"*Stop it*," she says more desperately now, and then, "I didn't want to say the real reason I need to leave." These last words come out in a rush.

"And what's that?" I say, looking up with a scowl.

She bites her lip, blinks twice, and then says, "You're not enough for me, Jace."

It takes a minute for her words to truly register, for their meaning to unfold in my mind. And when they do, I freeze. "I'm sorry?"

"I meant what I said about everything else," she explains, "but the real reason we can't be together is that we just don't fit. I'm sorry. I don't make the rules about these things, but there it is. You're too young, too coarse. Too reckless."

Her words hurt worse than that fucking bullet ever did, digging into the same fear that plagued me watching her question Gia through the window.

She's too good for me.

"Reckless," I echo. "I thought you said I was a hero."

"It's a kind word for a stupid waste," she snaps. "If you're that careless with your own life, how the hell can I trust you with my heart?"

Behind me, the heart monitor is making all the noises I can't seem to.

"I could never spend the rest of my life with you," she says coolly. "And now that you're well, I can tell you."

"Cat...*baby*. Please."

She takes in a sharp breath at the endearment, and I'm not sure what I see on her face. Confusion? Cruelty? Regret?

Pain?

But it disappears in an instant, leaving only the familiar face of the Ice Queen behind.

"Goodbye, Jace," she says and starts for the door. "I'm looking forward to your return to duty."

I don't rip out the IV after all.

I watch her leave. I watch her leave in my army shirt with her hair still tangled from our impromptu fuck. I watch her leave, and I can still taste her on my lips.

And for the first time since I was shot, I feel like I might die.

CHAPTER FIFTEEN

CAT

I have a meeting with the FBI, and it takes over nine hours.

Nine hours to detail all the evidence against Pisani, sift through her statement, and apply it to what we know. She used her mother's car as a way to deflect visibility, and she robbed all those other doctors' offices as a way to keep suspicion on the stolen televisions and not on the decommissioned medical equipment in her own place of work. The FBI is tracking down a boyfriend they think helped her with the physical aspects of the burglary, and they're also attempting to track down the cobalt itself.

Why a Vassar grad became a criminal is still a question the FBI will have to answer, although I think I saw a hint of the reason in Pisani's statement.

I couldn't find a job after graduation, not a single one. And then I finally found this office job, and it barely paid any of my bills, and it was so boring I wanted to die...

Very smart and very bored. Add in some money problems and a healthy dose of anger, and that's all it takes.

By the time the meeting is over, I feel ready for an entire bottle of wine. Maybe even two.

It's the first time since I transferred into investigations in the weeks after Frazer's death that I've missed being a patrol officer. Missed being spared the interminable meetings, missed the clean-burning energy of working hard and then burning off steam at a bar or in someone's bed after.

Of course, right now there's only one bed I want to be in, and I made damn sure I'd never be invited back.

It was for his own good, I tell myself for the millionth time since I broke Jace's heart a week ago. He wasn't listening to reason, he wasn't letting me do this *for him,* so I had to *make* him let me go. I had to find the things I knew would make him flinch and make him doubt. I had to hurt him so he'd accept that we had to end.

One day he'll thank me. One day he'll realize that I was the one mature and sacrificing enough to protect his chance at having a full life.

That it killed me in the process is inconsequential. What's important is that he has his future back, full of all the opportunities and new women he deserves. Full of time for him to meet his real soul mate and do things at the pace they're supposed to be done.

What's important is that I won't have to wait up at night for him anymore. I won't ever have to watch someone hand a folded flag to his mother. I won't have to miss him so much it feels like the muscles of my heart are tearing themselves in half.

Except.

That's exactly how I feel right now.

And when the FBI finally has everything they need from

me to formally assume responsibility for the case, I go home so my heart can tear itself open in peace. I curl up in one of Jace's shirts, smelling the achingly familiar scent of tea tree oil and leather.

It was for his own good.

But I think I may have shattered any hope of *good* being a part of my own life now, and even though it was worth it, I still have to mourn the cost.

I gave him his future...

And now mine is empty without him.

Captain Kim calls me a few days later to tell me that both Jace and I will receive commendations from the chief at a special ceremony next week. He also tells me that since the case is no longer ours, Jace will return to Russo's squad whenever he gets off medical leave.

I should be happy about this—I know I should—but I hang up the phone and stare at my suddenly-too-big desk and feel like I've been hit in the chest.

He'll probably be relieved that we'll be back to never seeing each other at work, but I'm not. I can't be. I've only just now realized it, but I was counting on having at least *this* with him. At least the perfunctory *hellos* and *goodbyes* and accidental brushes of elbows and feet as we jostled for space at the same desk.

It's selfish to want it. I broke a good man's heart, and I don't get to have him close to me anymore. The sooner he moves on, the better it is for him, but I can't stop the ache of grief that comes with it all. The gnaw of bitter loss. I just want him near me, even if I can't have him, even if it's better for him to meet other women and go live his life... The idea of not seeing those flashing gray eyes and that stern mouth, of not hearing that deep, rough voice...

Ah, fuck, it hurts.

It hurts so much I don't know how I'll survive it.

But survive it I must, and survive it I do for the next week. I bury my pain in work, coming in early and staying up late in an attempt to exhaust my body and my mind. In an attempt to keep the sadness at bay and make myself too tired to miss Jace at night. It doesn't work on either count, so I only succeed in making myself tired *and* miserable, which I feel like I deserve.

I resist the urge to call.

I resist the urge to visit, even after I hear he's been released from the hospital.

I resist the urge to throw myself at his feet and beg, beg, beg his forgiveness.

It's for his own good.

It's unfair that I have to be the strong one right now—the wise one—when all I want to do is curl up in his lap and have him play with my hair. When all I want to do is marry him and have lots of gray-eyed babies and spend the rest of our lives making each other breakfast and sharing the job we love.

Because, yes, I see that now. I thought I hated that he was a cop as well. I thought I could never live with it, but now that we're apart...I miss it. I miss having someone to talk over a case with, someone who understands the uniquely exhausting and exhilarating parts of the job. I miss having someone to share it with.

All this tired unhappiness makes me jittery and anxious on the evening of the commendation ceremony. I pull on my dress uniform and pin on my brass with trembling fingers, and I don't bother to apply lipstick because I know I'll make a mess of it. And all because the man I love and had to push away will be there too.

Get it together, Cat.

But I can't. My stomach is hollowed out and my pulse is pounding when I get to the central station and walk inside. It's like every beat of my heart is saying *Jace, Jace, Jace.*

I'm sorry, I'm sorry, I'm sorry.

I detest these ceremonies anyway. They're anemic and bureaucratic and pointless. I already have several commendations on my wall. I've already gone to this same small reception room six times in my career and shaken the chief's hand and received a signed piece of paper I'll never look at again.

And now I'll have to go and do all this for the case that both brought me to Jace and also nearly got him killed?

It's very tempting to take this heavy dress hat off and go back to my car. Tempting just to walk away from it all—the ceremony and the memories and the inevitable agony I'll feel when I finally lay eyes on the man I love.

The man I hurt.

But it's not in my nature to shirk my duties, even if I think the duty pointless, so I keep the hat on and enter the reception hall, not surprised to see that it's only half full, and that half is all Jace's family.

His mom looks over her shoulder at me as I walk in, and

a flush rises to my cheeks, wondering if she hates me now that I've hurt Jace. Wondering if she now sees me as the predator I initially feared she would.

Her face opens in a smile, and she gives me a small wave, her husband doing the same, and I manage a nod back as my heart squeezes. Even still, I want his family to like me. How foolish is that?

There is, of course, nobody here for me. It's much too trivial to ask my parents to come over from France, and I don't have anyone else. No siblings. No close friends.

A bolt of loneliness hits me so hard that I can barely keep my back straight...and that's before I see him standing in front of me. Because when I see him, I think I might drop to my knees.

He's shaved for the ceremony, exposing fully that bladed jaw and that solemn, sensual mouth, but his hair is longer than he normally keeps it, dark and just a little messy, practically begging for my fingers to sift through it. The long-sleeved dress shirt stretches across his broad shoulders, testing the seams, and then the fitted fabric hugs the lean lines of his torso and waist. The tailored pants fit him almost indecently well, showing off narrow hips and long, powerful thighs, and even with his wounded arm up in a sling, he's still all potent, dominant male.

And when his fierce gray eyes lock on me, I know exactly whom he wants to dominate.

My body answers immediately, obedient to his silent command, and my nipples harden against the silk of my bra. I hope the thick fabric of the uniform is enough to conceal my response, but I know there's no hope for the blush on my cheekbones or the dilation of my pupils. He owns even the automatic responses of my body. He owns everything. So much so that even in front of this small crowd, I want to drag him off by his uniform tie and mount him in the first empty room we find.

No, Cat.

For his own good, remember?

And anyway, his desire is fueled by his palpable anger with me. I can feel it radiating off him, seething, lustful hurt, and God help me, it makes me want him more than ever. I want all of that possessive, revengeful man over me and underneath me. Claiming me. Destroying all my fears that he'll one day want a younger woman, obliterating my fear for his safety with the primal, urgent proof of his life.

I want to surrender the responsibility of doing the right thing. I want him to be the one to make all the hard choices now, and I want him to choose me.

I want to tell him I love him and that I'm sorry.

It hurts to tear my eyes from his, but I manage, approaching my chair and sitting without acknowledging him, which he scowls at. He also takes his seat, his long legs making it so our thighs brush briefly as he sits, and I can feel the shudder run through him as we touch. See his entire body quiver in ferocious restraint as the chief begins talking to the crowd.

Minute by minute, my resolve lessens and my famous ice thaws. I can smell that masculine scent of clean leather and tea tree oil. I can see his clenched thigh next to my own and those huge hands white-knuckled where they rest in his lap.

I'm weak, I'm so weak, because I want to beg his forgiveness and beg him to make me atone with my body, but I can't. *I can't.*

Dammit, Cat, you can't.

"...and that's why we're proud to present Officer Jace Sutton and Detective Catherine Day with these commendations. Let's give them a round of applause, shall we?"

We stand up, and then there's handshakes and pictures with the chief formally presenting us our commendation, and then finally, thankfully, it's over.

I bolt out of the reception room as fast as I can because I don't trust myself around Jace a moment longer. If I so much as look at him, speak to him, I'm going to crumble. I'm going to beg him to *make* me crumble, and if I'm going to survive losing him, I have to hold on to my pride somehow.

So I leave while he's talking to his family and take a shortcut through the employee-only hallway back to the parking lot, breathing a sigh of relief when the door closes behind me. This is the hallway where most of the civilian employees and administrative personnel work, and since it's evening, they've all left and I'm alone.

I need to get home. I need to get home where I'm safe from my own weaknesses, where I can burn off this need for Jace Sutton with a long run and a good toy and not by finding him and fucking myself on his angry erection until we're both too exhausted to move.

A door creaks; I stop and turn.

Jace is framed in the doorway like a wrathful god, striding

toward me with a look on his face that would signal to any other woman to take cover.

It only makes me ready for him, so ready that I ache. I'd do anything right now to ease that ache, any undignified thing, oh God oh God—

"We're going to talk now," Jace says, reaching me and yanking me into him with his good arm. Every curve of mine presses against his hard body, and the unmistakable proof of his wanting to "talk" digs into my belly. "We're going to talk until I fucking understand why you said the things you said that night."

I close my eyes in regret, in uncertainty. If I tell him I hated the things I said, that they were lies I chose for the plain fact that I *needed* to hurt him, then everything else will tumble out after it. How much I love him, how much I want him and want him to be mine.

And if he knew that? If he knew he had permission to claim me forever?

Then all of this would have been for nothing, and I wouldn't have saved him or myself from all the pain waiting for us in the future.

It's remembering the awaiting pain—inevitable, unavoidable—that gives me strength. I open my eyes and gaze up at his face.

"I said them because I had to," I say, which is not a lie.

Jace's eyes narrow. "You said them to hurt me. Every day, I thought you'd call to explain more, to tell me you were lying. To tell me I wasn't just..."

"Just what?" I whisper.

He exhales forcefully. "Just a young, dumb fuck. Just a good body for you to ride until you got bored."

I want to close my eyes again. I hate myself for giving him this doubt, this *wound,* but what else could I have done?

His face changes when I don't deny it right away, his defensive expression pulling into a dark scowl. "If that's all you want," he says roughly, "I can give it to you. You want me to fuck you like I did that first night, hmm? Bend you over the table and take what I need? Or what about the night I found you with Kenneth? What about the night I tore up your pretty silk blouse and tied you up with it so I could fuck your virgin ass?"

Despite all my regret and torment, his words stir up my already primed body, and I can't help the little moan that leaves my lips. His eyes flare, and suddenly I'm spun around, my hands pinned to the wall and my ass yanked back to his lap.

"I knew it," he breathes in my ear as his hand works at the belt to my dress pants. "Knew you wanted me."

I recognize distantly that I need to stop this, that I need to tell him my decision still stands no matter what, but dammit, I don't *want* my decision to stand! And how can I deny my neglected body what it's been keening for since I left him in that hospital room?

Instead, I grind back against his cock and whimper the moment his hand slides into my panties, his middle finger finding my clit with unerring accuracy and rubbing me so perfectly that I feel the climax already pulling tight in my belly.

"Yeah," he grunts behind me, rocking his clothed erection against me as he fingers me with that blunt male prerogative that gets me so hot. "That's it. Remind me how wet and tight that pussy gets for me. Remind me how hard I make it come."

I've been too long denied, too desperate, and his words eradicate any barrier between me and what he demands of my body. In a sharp, vicious instant, I come so hard my knees buckle and it's his hand on my cunt keeping me upright.

"Need to fuck you," he mumbles into my hair. "Need it."

"Yes," I breathe, still riding it out on his hand. "Yes, please, yes."

He pulls his hand free, and then I hear the unmistakable noise of him sucking his finger clean. It's so carnal and raw that I think I might pass out from craving alone, from needing that massive cock stroking inside me—and then he uses his damp fingers to gently brush my hair away from my neck so he can kiss the sensitive skin there. That combination of dirty and tender that undoes me, every single time.

I can feel him reaching for his belt, unfastening it one-handed and then tugging at his zipper. I arch my back, thinking I'll yank my own pants down around my hips just so I'll be ready when he is—and then he stops. Hand on his zipper, his lips against my nape, he goes completely still.

"Please," I whimper. I'll die if he doesn't give it to me. "Jace."

He shivers at my plea, but then the ragged inhale he sucks in tells me his shiver wasn't one of pleasure.

"I can't," he says after a moment. "I won't."

He's there behind me, erect and unzipped, and I'm wet from the frantic, heated orgasm he just gave me in the hallway of a police station...

...and it's not going to happen.

He's not going to fuck me. There's not going to be some kind of electric connection that fixes everything between us. No frenzy of sweat and need that absolves us of past sins and leaves us clean and ready for a new future on the other side.

I'm frozen in place, my hands still spread against the wall like I'm being frisked, and I don't know what to say or what to do. I don't know what he needs or what I need. I don't know how to make this okay between us, how to get back to where we were before I defaced it with my fears.

Oh God. *I want things to go back to the way they were?*

What does that even mean?

His hand fists at my shirt near my shoulder, keeping me close to him. "I want to," he murmurs against my neck. "*Fuck,* I want to. And I thought maybe...maybe if this was the only way you'd take me, then I'd give it to you, because that's how much I want you in my arms. But I—" He takes a determined breath, his chest swelling against my back. "But I can't do that to us, and I won't cheapen what I feel for you."

God, how is he so *good*? So good even now, after I've hurt him? After I've shut him out? Maybe I've been wrong about which one of us is the mature one, the wise one. Maybe I should have trusted Jace's faith in us from the beginning...

He lets me go with a finality that makes me wince, zipping up and buckling his belt all before I can manage to turn to face him.

Fix this! my heart demands, but I don't know how. I don't know if I can.

And it doesn't matter because Jace is right in front of me,

but he may as well already be out the door. His silver gaze is filled with pained resignation.

"It was never something tawdry or transactional on my end," he says quietly. "In fact, I always believed you were the best thing to have ever happened to me."

A choked noise echoes in the hallway, and I only realize it came from me when I feel a hot tear trace down my cheek to my jaw.

"And now I know," he continues, just as quietly, "that you never believed the reverse."

"Jace," I say, more tears coming now. "Stop. Please, that's not—"

"It's okay," he says, running his hand over his face. "It's okay. I can't make you love me like I love you, and you know what? I don't want to *make* you. I thought I could prove to you that you were mine. I thought I could possess you with my body, and that would be enough—but I don't want to possess you if you don't want to be possessed, you know? It's only worth calling you mine if you say it right back to me. And I know what happened with Frazer was fucked up, I know me getting shot was terrifying, but there's got to be a time when you choose to move forward, no matter how scary it is."

He leans forward and kisses my forehead, and my mind—normally the sharp, focused tool I prize—fails me. I'm searching through his words for an answer, searching through my own thoughts, and it's so hard because I'm crying and I can't see, and all I can do is slump back against the wall and try to breathe. Try to live.

Because what is he really asking me?

For the truth and an apology, almost certainly, but I think he's asking me for more. I think he's asking me to take a risk, to relinquish control...to be vulnerable.

To thaw.

Ever since Frazer died, I've been doing everything I can to keep myself as frozen as possible. Deep down, I never really minded being called Officer Ice Queen. I was a little proud of it, in fact, because it meant I did what I needed to. It meant I succeeded in keeping myself safe and my heart protected.

It meant I was strong.

But now?

Is this the kind of strong I want to be? The kind of strong that hurts other people "for their own good"? The kind of strong that would rather push someone away than do the hard work of loving through fear?

God, no. Maybe I needed these last twelve years of control. Maybe being an island has served me in the past, but not anymore. Not anymore because I have Jace and I have the knowledge I've had all along but somehow still couldn't believe until now: surviving isn't living.

And I'd rather be vulnerable with Jace than strong without him.

My breath catches, my heart pounding with this epiphany and my fingers already flexing to grab him back to me, to pull him close and tell him everything.

To tell him I love him and I want to move forward with him, even though, yes, I'm scared.

But when I wipe the tears from my eyes, I see something awful. I see that I'm alone.

Jace is gone.

CHAPTER SIXTEEN

JACE

My instincts have never failed me.

Not in a war zone, not on the beat. Not even when I took a bullet in a medical building staff room, because taking that bullet meant Cat was safe. Which means I'd do it a thousand times over again if I had to, even knowing how the shooting unraveled into pain and heartbreak. I'd still choose it because keeping her safe is the priority.

No, my instincts have never failed.

Except for right now.

I walk out to my car with fast, jerky strides, desperate to avoid anyone lingering after the ceremony or the usual flow of evening-shift cops dropping off in-custodies or hopping into the report room to catch up on paperwork. I smell like Cat and my uniform is rumpled, and I can't decide if I need to cry or smash something with my fists. So yeah, avoidance seems like the right strategy.

And as I go, I question myself over and over again. How could I have been so wrong about us? How could my instincts have let me down?

From the moment I first saw that woman, I knew she was

mine. Knew we fit together in some important way I didn entirely understand yet. And truly, through the next near month we shared, I saw our fit become better and better. She laughed more, played more. She trusted me, shared that keen mind with me, shared moments of genuine, unfiltered joy.

I knew she was good for me in every measurable way. But hell, I thought I was good for her too. I *needed* to be good for her. Not because of my male ego—well, okay, not *only* because of my male ego—but because she deserved it. She deserved someone to be good for her. Because it felt wrong to sponge up all that intelligence and determination without giving her something in return.

All of that came crashing down that awful night in the hospital, of course, but there'd been some stubborn part of me that refused to believe she really meant the things she said. This silly, fragile hope that she would confess she'd pushed me away out of fear and wanted to make it right.

Too young, too coarse.

A stupid waste.

Even now, the words rake over an unhealed wound, but even in my pain and shock that night, even through her cruel tone, I heard something almost sad in her voice when she accused me of being reckless.

If you're that careless with your own life, how the hell can I trust you with my heart?

Yes, I'm young, and yes, I'm probably coarse and reckless and everything else she said—but I know the woman I love. I know she's afraid and afraid with good reason. I know she's kept herself safe for a long time by keeping everyone else away.

And I thought tonight when I chased after her...

It doesn't matter. You were wrong. She didn't confess to any of that. She didn't apologize. She simply offered me her body. As if that were any kind of substitute for her heart. So now, here I am, alone and torn up and forced to acknowledge I was wrong about all of it.

She's not mine, and she never was.

When I get in my car, I'm not even sure where I want to go. My apartment is still haunted by her. By the few odds and ends she left there. By the tea I bought for her and by the memories of her presence. I don't feel like seeing any of my family or friends, and I don't really feel like getting a drink at the Dirty Nickel and watching whatever sports thing is on the television there. Every place I can think of feels wrong because every place I can think of is a place without her.

I finally decide to hit the gym. It's attached to my duty station up north, and I've got a change of gym clothes in my locker. Better yet, since it's only for cops, it's usually only got one or two other people in it, and I'll have a chance at some privacy while I try to burn out these feelings.

I try not to let myself think too much as I drive from the main station to my station. I try not to think about Cat's silence when I laid myself bare for her or about how she didn't correct me when I told her I knew she didn't love me like I loved her.

I try not to think about her at all.

And fail miserably.

♦ ♦ ♦ ♦

An hour later, I'm sweaty and ragged, having set the treadmill to a dead sprint and then pounding out a run like I was being chased by ghosts, my arm wound screaming like hell the whole time. I grab my reusable water bottle and start chugging as I leave the gym and walk down the short hall to the locker room. Even though my body is thirsty and beat, my mind is still chewing on itself, wondering where I went wrong, and my chest still feels like it's been cracked wide open.

I strip off my clothes—miserably, tugging on the waterproof sleeve over my bicep to protect the bandage there—and then I shower—also miserably, too messed up to even touch the swelling erection my starved cock is offering up against the water. Even fatigued, my body remembers that just ninety minutes ago I had Cat pressed against me, ready and whimpering for me to slide inside her. Even heartbroken, my flesh still aches for hers.

With a long, weary sigh, I shut off the shower and wrap a towel around my waist. I slide the curtain aside with a vicious gesture, scowling down at my unrepentant cock.

"Jace. Look at me."

My heart stops. The air turns to concrete in my lungs. I look up and see the woman I love in front of me, still in her dress uniform, her aqua eyes like oceans of feeling and her Hollywood hair still tousled from where I kissed it earlier. Despite everything, my stomach flips over with an idiotic, naïve flip. I still want to see her. I still *want* her even though I know better, and it's frustrating as hell.

"What do you want?" I ask, irritated that the words come out husky and curious when they should come out cold and flat. But I can't help it. I can't help anything about how I feel about Cat. She could rip out my heart with her bare fingers and eat it in front of me, and I'd still want to pull her into my arms.

But she doesn't look like she's come here to eat my heart. Instead, she's sinking her teeth into her bottom lip and twisting her slender fingers in the department-issue necktie she's wearing with her dress uniform.

She looks...well, *nervous.*

But every second she doesn't speak reminds me that I'm damp and wearing nothing but a towel—and that towel has an oblivious erection twitching underneath it—and I finally say, "Look, we can talk later—"

"I haven't told you everything about Frazer's death," she blurts out before I can finish.

Her eyes widen fractionally, as if she can't believe she really just said those words, but then she takes a deep breath and forges on while I stand frozen in my towel. "That night—that call—I got there first. The dispatch notes said someone heard a woman screaming inside. Now we know it was the perp screaming, but then we thought it was someone else he was hurting..."

She trails off, and I nod because I know. Lots of situations require backup—but sometimes they require an officer's immediate intervention more. If she thought someone was in danger, of course she would have gone in alone. I would have too.

But that doesn't stop my pulse from spiking with worry, no matter how long ago this happened, and I think I possibly understand how Frazer felt when he realized she'd gone in there without him.

"The power had been turned off. I told you that, but did I tell you how hard it was raining that night? Flash floods all over town. The streets were like rivers. Every other step I took, there was a clap of thunder or a fresh gust of wind. Scared even me, and when I found the perp, he was huddled in the back room, crying and frightened. Abject, utter terror. Hearing him cry like that was...bone-chilling."

Cat takes another deep breath and looks at the ceiling to gather herself. "I started talking to him. It took a minute or two, but he began to settle down. He told me it wasn't a storm at all but people trying to kill him, and he was so, so scared. Had a kitchen knife with him in case 'the people' made it into the house. But I managed to get him to set it down, managed to get him to make eye contact, was able to say over the radio that the subject was alone and compliant and that we were in the back bedroom."

"But then Frazer..."

A tear spills over Cat's eye, and she wipes furiously at it as she nods. "He kicked in the back door—maybe because he thought it would be closer to the bedroom? If he'd just entered through the front door, which I'd already broken open, or if he'd just trusted that I'd call out on the radio if I needed help..."

"Cat, it was the suspect he didn't trust, not you."

She shrugs, and I know she thinks the distinction doesn't matter. And maybe it doesn't. The outcome was the same, after all.

"It startled the suspect. He grabbed his knife and pushed past me and went down the hall toward the noise. It was so dark, so fucking dark, and I tried to follow him, but I was tripping over all the trash in the hallway, and I—" Another tear, but she doesn't flinch away from her next sentence. "I was too late."

Her words hang in the cool, damp air of the locker room. I give her time to find her next words.

"He didn't have to die," she finally whispers. "Nobody had to. If only he'd waited or taken a minute to think and come through the front...he might still be here with me."

Oh God. Suddenly I see exactly where this is going. "I'm not Frazer."

She shakes her head. "No. No, I know you're not. I can't fault Frazer for trying to keep me safe, and I can't fault anything you did with Pisani either. But I'm just trying to explain...why..."

I soften. "I know *why*, baby. It's never been a secret to me."

She looks down at her hands, still twisting in her tie. "I just thought if I didn't let anyone in, then they'd be safe. And I let you in...and you got shot. You did the same thing he did, and you rushed in and you almost got killed. You can see why that's hard for me."

I wince. I hate how this is between us, this mountain of causality. This reality of our job, jagged and insurmountable. "Cat."

She doesn't let me cut in; she keeps going. "But you know what? I'm tired of the hard things keeping me from what I really want. I'm tired of the walls and the precautions and the ice. I was wrong, Jace. Wrong about what I wanted."

Her words hit me good and hard, like a cold shot of top-shelf vodka. I think I feel those words buzzing in my veins.

"What do you mean?" I ask, voice rough. "Say what you mean."

Her eyes are the sweetest sea color, and she gives me a sad, pleading smile that makes me want to slay monsters for her, even if the monsters are the sins between us.

"I mean I'm sorry for the things I said," she says. "They were lies, Jace. The worst lies I could think of to make you let me go. I'm too selfish to want you to find a better, younger woman. I want you with *me.* I want to be your woman, age be damned."

I can't help the hope swelling in my chest like a balloon, and I take a step forward, reaching for her. She lets me. She lets me pull her into my chest with my good arm, and then she tilts her head back to look up into my face.

"I mean I love you," she says softly, her hand coming up to cup my jaw. "You're too young and too brave and so very caveman—and I love you. I love you so much that I'm willing to be scared. I'm willing to be vulnerable. I love you so much that nothing else matters."

"Babe," I rumble, burying my face in her hair as I squeeze her even closer to me. "Babe. Nothing else does matter. It never did to me."

"Oh, Jace. Can you forgive me? The terrible things I said?"

"I already have," I say, and I mean it. It's the truth.

"And pushing you away? Leaving?"

"You're here now, and that's all that matters to me." I kiss her hair again, never able to get enough of that delicate silk against my lips, of that exquisite, expensive scent of hers. "Fuck, I love you. And yes, I was hurt and angry and all the things when you left, but if you're willing to be open with me, then I'll be open with you. I don't see what we can't figure out if we have love and honesty."

I feel her smile against my chest. "So wise for one so young."

"Well, I stole that line from my PTSD counselor, but I still mean it."

She laughs. "Good."

She kisses my chest, and my cock responds, surging again under the towel and brushing against her. She purrs a little. "Young man."

And then she reaches under the towel to give me a firm, urgent stroke. My eyes flutter closed. "What happens next?" I manage to ask. "Do I get to take you home?"

"Every day for the rest of forever. But first..." Another stroke.

I groan.

"First," she whispers, "we're going to see how fast you can make this ice queen melt."

Game. On.

EPILOGUE

JACE

A year later...

“At some point, you’re going to have to let me sleep, caveman,” Cat teases, but she parts her pretty thighs for me all the same as I walk toward the bed.

“We’ll sleep in tomorrow,” I promise, giving my already primed cock a few slow strokes. Even though I just came back from putting away the warm cloth I used to clean her, I’m ready again. It’s our third fuck of the night because I can’t fucking get enough of her right now. I mean, I never have anyway, but right now, with my ring glinting on her finger and her belly heavy with our first child, I’m more caveman than ever.

“We have to work on the nursery tomorrow,” she reminds me, idly plucking at her nipple as she watches me approach. “We should rest...”

But her sensible words are canceled out by the hungry way she watches my cock bob up and down as I climb onto the bed.

“No rest for the wicked, babe,” I say, even though she is right about the nursery. I moved into her house when we t married half a year ago, and we've only just now finished ntegrating my things and turned to making the baby's room ready for his entrance in four more months.

"I suppose we have time," she muses, her free hand going between her legs to toy with the place I've already thoroughly pleasured tonight...and plan on pleasuring again.

I grunt in agreement as I mount between her thighs and take myself in hand.

"*Young* man," she sighs happily, petting my hard abs and sliding her palms up the flexed lengths of my quads. "My young stud."

And then her sigh turns into a broken moan as I slide on inside. She's wet and swollen from all our earlier play, which makes her slick as hell and tight as a fist. She cradles her own breasts as I give her a second, deeper thrust, and the sight of her hands plumping and squeezing her own tits is almost too much.

"Shit, babe," I mutter. "Gonna go fast if you do that."

She just gives me a sly smile and continues the show, driving me to a state of indecent desperation and making my own palms itch to feel her. With a growl, I pull out and move us so I'm lying behind her, my chest to her back and my cock prodding at her sweet pussy from behind. I nip at her neck as I flex my hips and search out her tits with my own hands.

"Mine," I grunt.

"Yes," Cat gasps, arching so that her ass is pressed against my lap and her breasts press even harder into my hands. "All yours."

Her curves are irresistible like this, and my hands can't

stop their possessive roaming as I take my time fucking her. I love the heavy weight of her tits now that they're growing full for our baby. I adore the swell of her belly that I helped create. I love them all so much that I tell her I'm going to have five more babies with her, maybe seven or eight even, because I just love it so much.

Funny how she was afraid that I'd balk at having to choose a family too soon. If she'd asked me, I would have told her the truth.

Nothing with her is ever too soon.

She's been horny as hell since I knocked her up, and it takes her almost no time to come again, writhing back against me and working my cock inside her to wring out every last bit of pleasure. When she finally settles, limp and satisfied, I wrap her tight in my arms, pull her ass flush to my lap, and rock into her with slow, grinding slides, feeling my shaft thicken with the inevitable.

"Give it to me, Officer," she whispers. "Every last drop."

She doesn't have to tell me twice. With another ferocious growl, I release all my love and passion into her, spurting hot and thick and wet inside her channel and flexing my hips to get deeper as I do.

I've come enough already tonight that this climax has a bite to it—a sharp ache with every dizzying pulse, and I love it. I love knowing the ache comes from making her mine over and over again. From claiming her body so thoroughly that we're both spent and sweaty. And I finish my claim now with a bite on her neck. Not enough to truly hurt but enough so she feels her caveman marking her on her skin and inside ıer body at the same time.

It feels so fucking good to empty inside her with my arms holding her tight, so good that my orgasm goes on and on and on, until finally I'm completely drained and not a little sore. I slide free with a kiss to her shoulder and go to get a fresh rag. When I come back, she's got her hand on her stomach and her aqua eyes are wide with delight.

"Jace," she murmurs. "I think you might be able to feel him from the outside now."

I practically sprint to the bed, touching where she is. I've been dying to feel the baby move, to feel all the little kicks and rolls that she's already been able to feel. And sure enough, after a long, quiet moment, I feel the slightest, faintest movement against my palm. And then again. And then again.

I'm smiling like an idiot, I know, but I don't even care. That balloon of hope I felt on the day Cat came back to me is so big in my chest, I think I might float away. I think I might already be floating.

"That's our baby," I say in awe.

"That's our baby," she says. "Still want to have seven or eight?"

"More," I tease, nipping at her ear and finally cleaning her. "I want you pregnant all the time."

She rolls her eyes, but her little smile tells me she's in on the joke. I want us to have the right size family for us, whatever that looks like and however we can balance it with both of us wearing badges. And while I jest that I want as many babies as she'll give me, she also knows I'm content with any future of any kind. More than content, I'm ecstatic. I'm married to the smartest, bravest, strongest woman in the world. Why wouldn't I be?

Cat likes it when I exercise my "male prerogative," as she calls it, so when I finish cleaning her, I tuck her close to me and kiss her head and make all sorts of primal promises about what I'm going to do with her body as soon as we've rested up a little. And then she falls asleep, snoring sweetly on my bicep with my other arm cradling her pregnant belly and her strong heartbeat thrumming under my palm.

No, this could never happen too soon. In fact, when it comes to this stunning, clever woman, nothing can ever happen fast enough.

ALSO AVAILABLE FROM

WATERHOUSE PRESS

Keep reading for an excerpt!

EXCERPT FROM
MISADVENTURES AT CITY HALL

"Do you really work in this building? Here at City Hall?" He leaned against the wall with one shoulder and looked down at me. Even with my pumps on, he was still a few inches taller.

"No. I was just riding the elevator up and down a few times for a cheap thrill. We don't have those fancy things where I come from." What could he possibly think I was doing in this building on a weeknight, exactly at quitting time, with a briefcase and a handbag dangling from my shoulder?

Kyle shook his head slowly from side to side. "My God, you're a handful. So refreshing. Let's try this a different way. See if you can manage an appropriate response to *something*." He stood up straight from the wall and dramatically adjusted his posture and suit. He reached into the pocket on the inside of his coat and pulled out his business card.

Extending his hand in greeting, he said, "Hello. I'm Kyle Armstrong. I work in the assistant district attorney's office, specifically in special operations as the grand jury advisor."

I shook his hand and took the little card as a slow smile

spread across my lips. This guy was too much, and I realized Bailey was spot on with her opinion of my poker face. It sucked.

"Well, it's nice to meet you, Grand Jury Advisor Armstrong," I replied. "I'm Skye Delaney. I, too, work in this old pile of bricks and mortar. Just a few floors up in the mayor's office. I'm the assistant to the city manager."

"Impressive, Ms. Delaney. No wonder you have such a bad attitude all the time."

"I beg your pardon?" I looked up from his card, which I had been studying just so I wouldn't be staring at his gorgeous face.

"Well, working for those old buzzards can't be very much fun. At least until recently, with all the drama you've had up there," he added.

"Well, I go to work to get my job done, not to have fun. But, as *fun* as this little run-in has been, I need to be off. I'm meeting someone." I walked toward the elevator to press the call button and he stepped in front of me, blocking my path.

I looked up at him impatiently.

"You're meeting someone? Tonight?" His voice took a darker tone where it had just been playful moments before.

"That's what I just said. I would think if it's your job to deal with grand juries, you'd pay closer attention when people speak. No?" I stretched around his tight backside to press the button, but he wouldn't budge. "Move your ass so I'm not late."

He stepped to the side and I pressed the down arrow.

"Why don't I go with you?" he asked hopefully.

"For starters, you haven't been invited. Secondly, I'd like to enjoy my evening. And you, Mr. Assistant District Attorney slash special ops slash grand jury advisor are a giant pain in my ass."

Untrue on so many levels.

In some unexpected combination of moves, he spun me around and caged me between his long arms and the frame of the elevator, giving me nowhere to move except against his firm—*and Christ, I mean really firm*—body.

"Dude. No way." I tried pushing on his chest, but it was like pushing on a brick wall. "You can't do this shit here. We both work here," I whispered loudly in case anyone came around the corner to use the elevator.

"You're making me act irrationally. I don't know what you're doing to me, but I know I don't want you to walk away from me again right now," he said, leaning in closer. The faint scent of his cologne still lingered on his skin, teasing my senses with an exotic blend of spices.

"Haven't you learned by this point in life that you don't always get what you want?" I finally summoned enough courage to look up into his eyes. I had them imprinted in my memory from the night before, and they were still every bit as mesmerizing.

"Are you going out with another man tonight?" His tone dropped to an edgy, serious one.

"Yes. There will be a man there." No need to explain my relationship with Oliver. "But again, I need to point out how none of this is your concern."

"I can't let you go." He folded his fit arms across his

chest, and I quickly moved away from him.

"Do you hear yourself? We met last night. We made out in the middle of the street. We didn't elope. Get a grip, my friend." I was a little bit unhinged after being so close to that freaking body again.

"I can't deal with you being with another guy. I haven't had a chance to...to—"

"Jesus Christ, do I even want to hear how you finish that sentence? What? Skin me alive and wear my flesh as a double-breasted dinner jacket?" I asked, my voice rising in volume and intent. "Or—or keep my severed head in your freezer?"

Thankfully we must have been the only ones left on the floor, because no one had come to the elevator the entire time we'd been standing here. I leaned against the wall again where this whole ridiculous conversation started. My equilibrium was way off kilter.

He chuckled. "You've been watching too many CSI episodes. I was going to say I haven't had a chance to properly take you out." He took two steps toward me and I froze. His amber eyes zeroed in on mine, keeping me in place while he spoke.

"Or make you dinner." This time his voice was quieter, deeper. Two more steps and he was pressing up against me.

Him.

Against me.

Against the wall.

"And then fuck you." His voice was somewhere between a scratch and a scrape. The only difference between the two being one leaves a mark while the other doesn't. This would definitely stick with me for a while. Likely until he made good on his words and the promising look that came along with them. Both of which had wetness rushing to my pussy like I hadn't felt in months.

Many, many months.

Kyle pressed his lips to the hollow just below my ear. That perfect, sensitive spot that made the hair on my arms stand on end and send a tingling sensation down my spine to dance across my clit.

"You want that too."

This story continues in *Misadventures at City Hall*!

ACKNOWLEDGMENTS

This book is forged out of fourteen years of marriage to a cop, and to that cop, I owe a tremendous debt for almost anything you can imagine goes into the writing of a story. From everything to how multiagency investigation works to how quickly a duty belt can come off, and then of course with all the life essentials like solo parenting and making sure the cats get fed, my husband made sure the family, the house, and the book all came out the other side of the writing process ready for inspection. Thank you, Sergeant Karate, for literally everything.

Thank you to my amazing editor, Scott Saunders, who not only kept my burglaries separate from my robberies but also kept the words clear and sensical and pretty. And a huge thank you to the incredible Waterhouse team that's shepherded Misadventures in Blue out into the wild: Meredith Wild, Robyn Lee, Haley Byrd, Jonathan Mac, and Amber Maxwell.

Thank you to my agent, Rebecca Friedman, for being a tireless champion, and to all the usual suspects who help me pull a book together: Ashley Lindemann, Candi Kane, Melissa Gaston, and Serena McDonald. Julie, Tess, NCP, Nana, Sarah—your friendship, advice, and beer fridges

(some beer fridges more metaphorical than others) are the reasons why I can keep going in this wacky world of ours.

And finally, thank you to whoever dressed Gillian Anderson in those amazing silk blouses in the three seasons of *The Fall*. One of these days, I'm going to write a book of hymns dedicated to her wardrobe, but for now, I've written a romance novel.

MORE MISADVENTURES

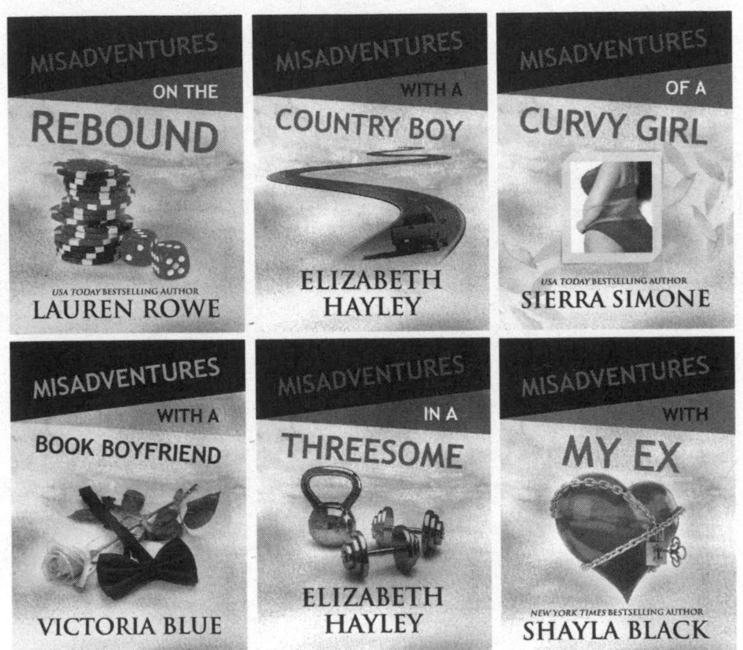

VISIT MISADVENTURES.COM
FOR MORE INFORMATION!

MORE MISADVENTURES

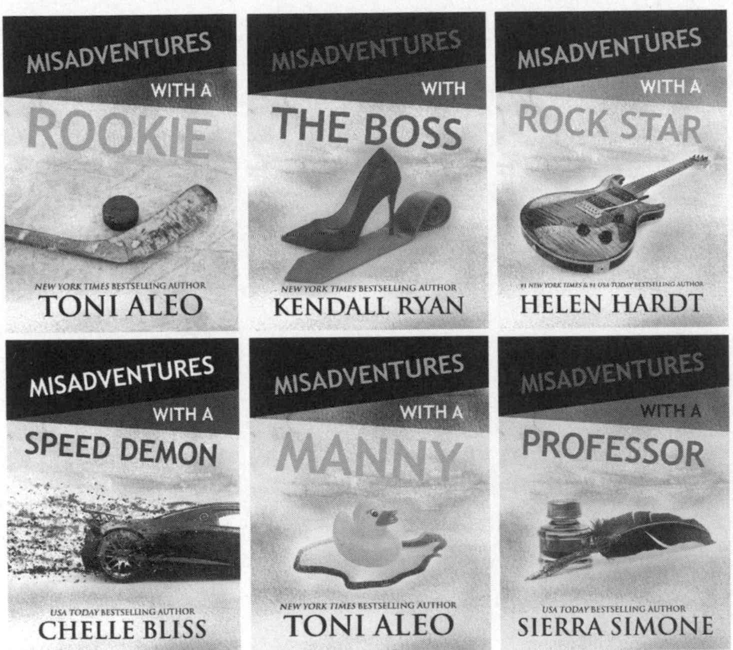